As the summer ap[...]
raise your temperature in Harlequin Presents!

Don't miss the first book in an exciting new trilogy, ROYAL BRIDES, by favorite author Lucy Monroe. *The Prince's Virgin Wife* is a tale of an irresistible alpha prince, an innocent virgin and the passion that ignites between them. In part two of Julia James's glamorous MODELS & MILLIONAIRES duet— *For Pleasure...or Marriage?*—enter a world of sophistication and celebrity, populated by beautiful women and a gorgeous Greek tycoon! *Captive in His Bed* is part two of Sandra Marton's Knight Brothers trilogy. This month we follow the passionate adventures of tough guy Matthew. And watch out, this story is in our UNCUT miniseries and that means it's *hot!*

We've got some gorgeous European men for you this month. *The Italian's Price* by Diana Hamilton sees an Italian businessman go after a woman who's stolen from his family, but what will happen when desire unexpectedly flares between them? In *The Spanish Billionaire's Mistress* by Susan Stephens, a darkly sexy Spaniard and a young Englishwoman clash. He thinks she's just out for her own gain—yet the physical attraction between them is too strong for him to stay away. In *The Wealthy Man's Waitress* by Maggie Cox, a billionaire businessman falls for a young Englishwoman and whisks her off to Paris for the weekend. He soon discovers that she is not just a woman for a weekend....

Check out www.eHarlequin.com for a list of recent Presents books! Enjoy!

Sandra Marton

CAPTIVE IN HIS BED

uNcut

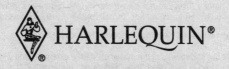

HARLEQUIN®

TORONTO • NEW YORK • LONDON
AMSTERDAM • PARIS • SYDNEY • HAMBURG
STOCKHOLM • ATHENS • TOKYO • MILAN • MADRID
PRAGUE • WARSAW • BUDAPEST • AUCKLAND

ISBN 0-373-12537-2

CAPTIVE IN HIS BED

First North American Publication 2006.

All about the author...
Sandra Marton

SANDRA MARTON wrote her first novel while she was still in elementary school. Her doting parents told her she'd be a writer someday and Sandra believed them. In high school and college, she wrote dark poetry nobody but her boyfriend understood, though looking back, she suspects he was just being kind. As a wife and mother, she wrote murky short stories in what little spare time she could manage, but not even her boyfriend-turned-husband could pretend to understand those. Sandra tried her hand at other things, among them teaching and serving on the board of education in her hometown, but the dream of becoming a writer was always in her heart.

At last Sandra realized she wanted to write books about what all women hope to find: love with that one special man; love that's rich with fire and passion; love that lasts forever. She wrote a novel, her very first, and sold it to the Harlequin Presents line. Since then, she's written more than sixty books, all of them featuring sexy, gorgeous, larger-than-life heroes. She's a four-time RITA® Award finalist. From *Romantic Times BOOKclub* she's received five awards for Best Harlequin Presents of the Year and a Career Achievement Award for Series Romance. Sandra lives with her very own sexy, gorgeous, larger-than-life hero in a sun-filled house on a quiet country lane in the northeastern United States.

PROLOGUE

High in the mountains of Colombia:

THE FOREST was dark.

The only sound was the roar of the waterfall.

The moon had risen, a fat, ivory globe that seemed suspended in the leafy branches of the trees. Its light illuminated the clearing and the jewel-like pool.

Illuminated Mia, standing naked under the frothy liquid veil of the waterfall.

He stood on the edge of the clearing, watching her and searching deep within himself for the discipline by which he'd lived his life, but that was the trouble.

He had no discipline when it came to her.

He'd searched for her, found her, then lost her.

Now, he had her trapped. She was his... Except, she wasn't. She'd made that clear. She had left him for another man. A man who'd wanted her back even though he said she had betrayed him.

Then, why would you want her? Matthew had asked, at the beginning.

It was an honest question. He'd understood that the woman would be beautiful—the man had shown him her photograph—but the world was filled with beautiful women. What made this one so special?

The man had looked embarrassed. He'd given a little laugh and said he wanted her back because she was more than beautiful.

She was, he'd said, everything a man could ever hope for.

Matthew felt his body quicken.

It wasn't true. She wasn't everything a man could hope for.

She was more.

He knew that now because, for a little while, she had belonged to him. She was Eve, she was Jezebel, she was Lilith reborn. She could be as wild as the summer lightning that streaked the hot sky or as sweetly gentle as spring rain.

Just looking at her was enough to stir a man's soul.

Her face was oval, her eyes wide-set and dark above an aristocratic nose and a mouth made for sin.

Her hair was long and dark as coffee. It tumbled down her back in a mass of curls that begged for his touch.

She was tall and slender, but her breasts were full and round. His breathing grew uneven at the thought of how they'd filled his hands.

And her legs…her legs were meant to clasp a man's waist. He could still remember the feel of them as he parted her thighs and sank deep, so deep into her heat.

Matthew shuddered.

God, was he losing his mind?

Who was Mia Palmieri? What was she? Was she his woman or Hamilton's? Had everything been a game?

All he knew right now was that she was a temptress.

But he was a warrior.

She swung toward him.

Matthew held his ground. She couldn't possibly see him. He was still dressed in black, the kind of stuff he'd worn on night maneuvers in Special Forces and then in the Agency. He knew that he blended in against the tangle of night-shadowed forest behind him.

Did she somehow sense his presence?

Was that why she was tilting her head back, lifting her face to the curtain of water? Why she was raising her hands, cupping her breasts as if she were offering herself to the gods?

Offering herself to him?

He was hard as stone. So hard that it hurt.

Once, he had promised to return her to the man who'd sent him to find her.

Tonight, his only promise was to himself.

Slowly he stepped forward into the patch of moonlight that swathed the little clearing. He waited, muscles tensed, willing her to look toward him again. Why? Why not just call out and let her know he was here?

The answer was a cold whisper inside his head.

Because he wanted to see what she did when she saw him. Would she run to him? Throw herself into his arms? If she did—God, if she did…

But she didn't.

Her reaction was like a kick in the gut.

Her eyes widened. Her lips parted on a little exclamation of surprise. She flung one arm across her breasts, the other over her feminine delta in an age-old gesture of modesty.

He knew damned well it was reflex action and nothing more, knew he had all the answers he needed… the answers he hadn't wanted.

"No," she said.

He couldn't hear the word but he could see her mouth form it. "No," she said again, and Matthew felt the swift rush of adrenaline as it coursed through his body.

His lips drew back in a predator's smile. He toed off his running shoes, pulled his shirt over his head, unzipped his trousers and stepped free of them.

Stood still, letting her see the full measure of his arousal.

Then he dove cleanly into the dark jungle pool and went for her.

CHAPTER ONE

Cartagena, Colombia, two weeks earlier:

MATTHEW KNIGHT sat at a table outside the Café Esmerelda, drinking a bottle of Colombian *cerveza* and wondering what in hell he was doing in Cartagena.

Years ago, in what he sometimes thought of as a different life, he'd left here and vowed he'd never return.

He'd even been in this café before, at this table, probably in the same goddamned chair, his back to the wall and his eyes sweeping the busy square, trying to spot trouble before it bit him in the butt.

Old habits died hard. So did memories that drove you from sleep in the middle of the night.

Better not to think about that now.

It was hot but then, it had always been hot in Cartagena. You came down to it, nothing had changed. The smells, the traffic. Even the crowd jamming the square. *Soldados* and *policia*, *touristas* loaded down with enough jewelry, wallets and cell phones to keep the pickpockets happy…

A man had to watch his ass in Cartagena.

He'd known that the first time. He'd thought he was

pretty good at it, too, but if he had been good at it—if he had been—

Damn it, he wasn't going there. The past was dead. So was Alita.

Matthew drained the last cold drop of beer from the bottle.

He was here now as a civilian, not as an operative of an agency where black was white and white was black and nothing was ever meant to be what it seemed.

And, at thirty-one, he had the world by the balls.

He was in his prime, a hard-bodied six-foot-four-inches with the chiseled bone-structure of his half-Comanche mother and the emerald-green eyes of his Texan father. A razor-thin scar angled across one high cheekbone, a souvenir of a winter night in Moscow when a Chechnyian insurgent had tried to kill him.

Women went crazy for that scar. "It makes you look so dangerous," a little blonde had whispered to him just a few nights ago, and he'd rolled her beneath him and, to her delight, showed her just how dangerous he could be.

And he was rich.

Fantastically rich, and not a penny of it had come from his old man. When your father had spent years ignoring you—except for the times he told you that you'd never amount to anything—that was one hell of a fine achievement.

What had made Matthew rich was Knight, Knight and Knight: Risk Management Specialists, the company he'd founded with his brothers. A year apart in age, they shared the same tough history.

A mother who'd died when they were young. A power-hungry father. Teenage rebellion, a few semesters of college followed by Special Forces and the

Agency. Life became one long adrenaline rush. Danger and beautiful women became Matthew's drugs of choice, though the women never lasted.

A warrior never let his emotions control him.

"¿Otra cerveza, señor?"

Matthew looked up and nodded. The beer was the only thing he still liked about Cartagena.

Five years ago, the Agency had partnered him with an undercover DEA agent and sent them here to infiltrate a drug cartel. Their cover was that they were lovers, looking for some money to set themselves up. They weren't, but Alita liked to tease him and say if she ever got into men, Matthew would be at the top of the list. And he'd say, yeah, yeah, promises, promises…

Somebody sold them out.

Four armed men snatched them off the street and drove them to a falling-down shack in the jungle. They beat Matthew until he lost consciousness. When he came to, he and Alita were tied to chairs.

Now you will learn how a man gives a woman pleasure, gringo, one of their abductors said, sending all four into gales of laughter.

Alita showed the courage of a lioness. Matthew fought the ropes that bound him but he was helpless to stop what happened.

When it was over, two of the killers dragged Alita's body outside. The third went with them, saying he needed to take a piss after such hard work. One man remained to guard Matt. He grinned, showed a mouthful of brown teeth and said he was going to prepare for the next round of fun.

He was bent over two lines of white powder just as Matthew finally freed his wrists.

"Hey, *amigo,*" he said softly.

The man turned and came toward him. In an instant, Matthew had his hand over the man's mouth and his arm around his neck. One quick twist and he was dead.

He killed two of the others with the dead man's weapon but only wounded the fourth. The guy ran into the jungle. Fine, Matthew thought coldly. A jaguar would make a feast of his flesh before the day ended.

He had other things to do.

Like burying Alita.

It was tough, not because it was difficult to scratch a grave in the fecund soil but because his eyes kept blurring with tears.

Standing over her grave, he vowed to avenge her.

He drove their abductors' car back to Cartagena, then to Bogotá. The embassy spook-in-residence debriefed him, expressed regret…and told him there would be no search for the killer who'd gotten away. When Matt demanded answers, his boss ordered him back to Washington.

Sheer luck had Cam and Alex in D.C., too. Over a bottle of Johnny Walker Blue, the brothers shared their disillusionment with the Agency.

Risk Management Specialists was born. Based in Dallas, the Knights provided their clients with solutions to difficult problems—solutions that were always moral if not exactly legal.

The Agency, and Colombia, became a memory…

Until now. Until Matthew's father asked him to meet an old friend with a problem. As a favor, he said.

Avery, asking a favor? Cam's recent brush with death had changed things. Matthew didn't entirely trust the change. Still, he'd agreed to the meeting. He'd listen to the guy's problem, maybe offer some advice. No way was he going to take on something that would keep him—

A man was coming toward him. Matthew took in the salient features. North American. Early forties. Good physical shape. Undoubtedly military, though he was in civvies.

"Matthew Knight?"

Matthew rose to his feet and held out his hand. "Yes."

"Douglas Hamilton. Sorry I'm late."

"No problem, Mr. Hamilton."

"It's Colonel." Hamilton's hand was soft, but his grip was strong. "I'm with the army." A quick flash of very white teeth. "The United States army. Didn't your father tell you?"

Matt motioned Hamilton into a chair, then signaled the waiter for two more beers.

"My father didn't tell me much of anything except that you and he are old pals."

Another flash of those white teeth. Matthew had seen sharks with similar smiles.

"Actually the friendship was between your father and mine." The waiter put down two icy bottles. Hamilton ignored his. "How is Avery?"

"Fine," Matt said politely, and wondered why he disliked Hamilton on the spot.

"I want to thank you for coming down here so quickly, Mr. Knight."

Matthew didn't answer. You learned more by letting silences grow than by hurrying to fill them.

"Trading on friendship is presumptuous but I needed a way to get to you." Hamilton paused. "You and your company have quite a reputation."

"You could have phoned. We're in the book."

Hamilton shook his head. "I couldn't discuss this on a telephone."

"Discuss what?"

"Straight to business. I like that." Hamilton's smile faded. "It's my fiancée. I'm afraid she's committed an, ah, an indiscretion."

Matthew sighed. Every now and then, somebody figured Knight, Knight and Knight for a detective agency.

"Colonel," he said politely, "I'm afraid you misunderstand what our company does. I'm not a private investigator. I don't deal in personal issues."

"I know that." Hamilton lowered his voice. "What I'm about to tell you must be kept in strictest confidence."

Hamilton's fiancée had slept with another man. That would surely be the so-called "indiscretion." Did Hamilton think he could hire a hit man? A couple of people had come to Risk Management with similar requests, but murder wasn't on their list of services.

"My fiancée became involved in—in something."

"An affair with another man?"

The colonel gave a harsh laugh. "I wish it were that simple." He hesitated, leaned closer. "She smuggled drugs."

Matthew blinked. "She smuggled—"

"Cocaine. As you know, diplomatic mail isn't subject to customs searches. Mia used my embassy privileges to send cocaine to the States."

Matthew stared at the man. It was a lot to take in. "Is she an addict?"

"Not as far as I know."

"Then, why did she do it?"

"For the money, I suppose. A lot of money."

"What happened when she was caught?"

"She wasn't. Not by the authorities. Someone tipped me off to what she'd done."

"Someone who owed you."

Hamilton smiled tightly. "You can put it that way, if you like. The point is, I took care of it."

Meaning, the colonel had used his considerable clout to bury the incident.

"I told Mia. I thought she'd be grateful. Instead, she was terrified. She said the people who owned the cocaine would think she'd cheated them and come after her."

"Well, she's probably right."

"I told her she'd be safe under my protection, but she didn't believe me. This was four days ago." Hamilton took a deep breath. "Yesterday, she disappeared."

The word made the hair rise on the nape of Matthew's neck. "Kidnapped?"

"Maybe. Or maybe she ran away. Either way, she's in terrible danger."

Matthew didn't bother disagreeing. "You've gone to the authorities," he said, even though he knew the answer.

"I can't. I'd have to tell them the whole story. Implicate Mia—"

"Implicate yourself."

The colonel didn't respond. He didn't have to. After a minute, Matthew nodded.

"I see your problem, colonel, but I don't understand how you think I can help."

"You can find her."

"That's out of the question."

"You know this country."

Matthew narrowed his eyes. "And you seem to know a lot about me."

Instead of answering, Hamilton took a photograph from his breast pocket and pushed it across the table.

"This is Mia."

Reluctantly Matthew picked up the photo and looked at it. He'd expected the colonel's fiancée to be attractive. A man like this wouldn't have a woman who wasn't, but Mia Palmieri had the kind of face and body that inspired painters and sculptors.

The picture had been taken on the beach on a day windy enough to have tossed her dark curls into a sexy mane and plastered her tank top to her high, rounded breasts. She wore shorts that showed off a pair of endless legs. Her eyes were wide and dark, her cheekbones sharp enough to etch glass, and her mouth…

Her mouth was made for sin.

A curl of desire knotted in Matthew's belly. It caught him by surprise.

"She's very attractive."

"She's beautiful," Hamilton said thickly. "More than beautiful. She's everything a man could want…and I want her back."

"Go to the authorities."

"I just told you—"

"You can't. Yes. You did tell me. And I'm telling you—"

"She's involved with the Rosario cartel. Does that name mean anything to you, Mr. Knight?"

Matthew's mouth thinned. "Why would it?"

"I checked your background. I know the story. You lost a partner. Can you stand by and let me lose my fiancée to the same people?"

A gust of wind snatched at the photo Matthew had left on the table. He caught it and looked at it again.

"Why did she try to smuggle coke?"

"I told you, I don't know."

"You said, for the money."

"Then why ask me again?"

"Maybe it was for kicks."

"What does it matter? She did it, and now—"

"Maybe she did it for you." Matthew smiled coldly. "Maybe you're the one behind the smuggling. Or maybe your fiancée wanted out of the relationship and that's why she split."

Hamilton's teeth clenched. "Are you accusing me?"

"I'm simply pointing out that if I start turning over rocks, there's no telling what I might find."

"You'll do it, then."

Matthew looked at the photo. He wished it had been taken at closer range. There was something in Mia Palmieri's eyes…

"Who saw her last?"

"My cook. She brought Mia lunch beside the pool. When she went back for the tray, the back gate was open and Mia was gone."

"I want to talk with the cook and the rest of your staff."

Hamilton's eyes glittered. "Thank you, Mr. Knight."

"Don't thank me until you have your fiancée back, Colonel." Matthew glanced at his watch. "I have a rented SUV. What's your address?"

Hamilton named a street high above the city, in one of Cartagena's most expensive neighborhoods.

Matthew nodded. "I'll meet you there."

Inside his rented Escalade, he took out the photo, held it against the steering wheel and stared at Mia Palmieri. The lady sure as hell didn't look like a drug smuggler, but Matthew's years in the Agency had taught him that the old adage was true.

You couldn't judge a book by its cover.

Still, there was something in her eyes...

He stared at the photograph for a long minute. For reasons he didn't understand, he stroked his thumb lightly over Mia's parted lips.

Then he turned the key, put the Escalade into a tight U-turn, and headed up into the hills.

Hundreds of miles away, in a hotel room high in the Andes, Mia Palmieri jerked upright from a restless sleep.

Something had brushed against her lips.

Heart pounding, she touched her mouth. There was nothing there.

Mia gave a little laugh. The breeze. That's what it was. Just the breeze from the open window.

She'd locked the door, put on the chain, even propped a chair under the knob, but she'd left the window open. Her room was on the second floor. It was safe enough.

Of course it was.

A minute crept by. Then she tossed back the covers, went to the window, closed and locked it.

Better, she thought.

Even so, it was more than an hour before she fell back into restless sleep.

CHAPTER TWO

W HERE WAS Mia Palmieri?

Had she run away, or had she been abducted? You got involved with people in the drug business, you played with fire. And that led to the next question.

Why would she have agreed to smuggle dope? The money was big but so were the risks, especially the way she'd done it. Using the embassy mail pouch had endangered not only her but her fiancé, too. Hamilton's prospects in the military were bright. You could almost see the yellow brick road that led straight to flag rank.

Why would she risk her future and his for something so risky?

Matthew had questions. Now, he needed answers.

A couple of hours later, they began trickling in.

Hamilton's house wasn't just expensive, it was well-guarded—but that wasn't uncommon in this part of the world. A wall topped by razor-wire surrounded the house; a gated run and kennel suggested that at least one guard dog roamed the property, probably at night.

Matthew identified himself at the gate. It swung open and he drove up to the house. The colonel greeted him and, at Matthew's request, walked him through the elegant rooms.

"Mia loved this house," the colonel said.

Maybe so, but the living arrangements left something to be desired.

The relationship between Hamilton and his fiancée wasn't normal. Not by Matthew's standards. If a woman who looked like Mia Palmieri had been part of his life, he damned well would have spent the nights with her in his arms

Not so the colonel.

He and his fiancée didn't share a room. Their rooms didn't even connect. Didn't adjoin. In fact, hers was in one wing of the colonel's expensive villa and his was in the other.

"You don't sleep together?"

Hamilton's face reddened. "Our sleeping arrangements are none of your business."

"Everything is my business now," Matthew replied. "Get used to it, Colonel."

"We slept together," Hamilton said stiffly. "Of course we did, but Mia…Mia insisted on her own room."

"Because? And please, Colonel, don't waste my time telling me she wanted her privacy."

He didn't know why he'd said that, but it worked. Hamilton's face reddened. "Mia's good at—at using sex to get what she wants."

"And what did she want from you, Colonel?"

Matthew knew the question was crude, but it was also deliberate. He wanted to see the colonel's reaction.

"It wasn't anything in particular. She just…" For a second, Matthew almost felt sorry for him. "She just thought it gave her control."

Matthew nodded. "And it did," he said softly. "She smuggled cocaine right under your nose."

"But I didn't let the drugs go through. I told you that."

"No. But you didn't make her face the consequences, either."

Hamilton's nostrils flared. For a minute, Matthew thought he was going to argue. Instead his shoulders slumped.

"I'm not proud of my weakness over Mia," he said quietly, "but I love her. And I want her back."

The cook confirmed that Mia had almost seemed to disappear into thin air. There'd been no sounds of a struggle, no overturned lounge chairs, nothing.

Anything else?

"Si," she said, after a couple of seconds. The *señorita* had left her lunch untouched. The only thing missing from the tray was a bottle of water.

Matthew found that interesting. Could a woman who'd been abducted without evidence of a struggle have the chance to take a bottle of water with her?

"Was anyone else working at the villa that day?"

"No, *señor,*" the cook said emphatically. Then she paused and said well, the pool boy had been there but when the *señorita* disappeared, he'd already gone to the house next door.

Matthew tracked the kid down. It took a few minutes but finally he recalled seeing a taxi drive past, maybe heading for the Hamilton place.

He drove into the city, stopped at a hotel, got a list of cab companies and lucked out on his third try.

For ten bucks, the dispatcher remembered he'd sent a taxi to the Hamilton address the day Mia disappeared.

Fifty bought the entire package: a meeting with the driver, who looked at Mia's photo and said *si,* yes, he remembered the lady.

He had taken her to a rent-a-car office.

The clerk at the rent-a-car counter remembered the lady, too. She'd asked for directions to Bogotá. The clerk had tried to talk her out of the trip. It was a long drive—fifteen, sixteen hours. And dangerous, especially for a *gringa.* But Mia had been insistent and the clerk had finally drawn the route on a map. The shortest route, she emphasized; at least the *señorita* had been smart enough to agree to that.

Half an hour later, Matthew was heading out of the city, but not on the road Mia had supposedly taken.

By now, he was sure she'd run away. The question was, why?

There were only two logical reasons. The first was that she was running from the cartel because the drugs she was supposed to smuggle hadn't reached their destination. That wouldn't have made them happy.

The second was that she was on the run with a cache of cocaine. That wouldn't have made the cartel happy, either. Cutting out the middleman wasn't their style.

It was the only logical explanation. A woman on the run, either from her boyfriend or from a pack of killers, would have taken the first plane out.

A woman on the run with a stash of stolen coke might very well try to lose any possible tail by driving into the mountains.

As for which route she'd take… The times he'd been on the run, he'd deliberately set up red herrings.

Maybe saying she'd take the short route was Mia's bit of misdirection. It was what he'd have done in her place.

He decided to go with his gut intuition and take the long way to Bogotá.

The road was rough but traffic was nonexistent so he made good time. He'd picked up a thermos of coffee and some sandwiches in Cartagena. When it grew dark, he pulled over and ate his makeshift supper. He was tired, couldn't remember the last time he'd slept or had a real meal, but Mia had a significant head start and he had to make up the time.

He stopped at each town, checked gas stations and inns, described her car and showed her photo. Nobody had seen her. A couple of hours before dawn, he took the Escalade down a rutted trail into a grove of trees, made sure his windows were locked, turned up the air conditioner and went to sleep with the nine millimeter automatic he always carried in his lap.

By the time the sun rose, he was on the road again, driving slowly along the early-morning streets of another town...

And spotted Mia's rental car outside a hotel that had seen better days.

Matthew pulled onto the patch of dirt that passed for a parking lot and went inside. He slapped the bell on the reception counter. After a minute, a door opened and a guy shuffled toward him, hair flapping in his eyes, shirt half-unbuttoned, his face contorted by a giant yawn.

Did the *señor* want a room?

Matthew gave him his best smile. *"Tengo una reserva,"* he said, meaning that he already had one. At least, he said, putting Mia's picture on the counter, his girlfriend had one. Trouble was, he couldn't recall the room number. Oh, and he didn't have a key, and he wanted to surprise her.

His performance was met with an unblinking stare.

He pulled some bills from his pocket and put them on the counter. The clerk palmed the bills and tossed him a key marked 204.

Matthew climbed the stairs. Went down a long, dim corridor to the corresponding door. Put his ear to the thin panel of wood and heard nothing.

Slowly he slid the key into the lock. Turned it. Eased open the door.

Mia wasn't there, but a woman's things were. A purse. A small suitcase, sitting opened on a chair. Clothes, laid out on the bed.

He could smell her scent, too. He'd noticed it in her bedroom at the villa. A softly feminine fragrance that made him think of a field of white flowers stretching to a pale blue horizon.

Matthew closed the door.

There wasn't much in the suitcase. No package of coke. Just a couple of T-shirts with the tags still on. The same for a pair of white cotton trousers. Some under-wear. Lingerie, she'd probably call it. Plain white cotton panties. An equally plain white bra.

Was that how Hamilton liked to see her? Or was it how she wanted him to see her?

A muscle danced in Matthew's jaw.

If she were his woman, he'd keep her in silk. Pale rose. Ivory. Shades to complement her dark hair and eyes. Silk thongs, to show off the curve of her hips. Silk bras, the kind that cupped a woman's breasts and made them an offering to her lover. Or ones that were sheer, so he could see the shadows of her nipples.

Matthew felt himself turn hard.

Hell, this was just what he needed. A men's magazine fantasy, doing its thing in his head over a woman who'd run away and left her lover to wonder if she were dead or alive. He didn't like Hamilton, his arrogance, his forced sincerity, but no man deserved to be treated like that.

Quickly he stripped the bed, checked it, checked under the mattress, checked the floor. He opened the dresser drawers. Empty. The same for the single drawer in the rickety nightstand. There was no closet, only a shelf, and all it held was a supersized spider.

If Mia Palmieri had dope, it was either on her or in her car. Okay. He'd check the car, then sit in his truck and wait for—

Footsteps were coming down the hall.

He went to the door and locked it. Then he flattened himself against the wall.

The footsteps came closer. Stopped, just outside. A key turned in the lock. The door swung open.

Matthew, lithe as a panther, had the door closed and locked, and his quarry trapped in his arms before she had time to react.

God oh God oh God...

Mia's breath rushed from her lungs.

A man's powerful arms closed around her from behind and lifted her into the air. She tried to scream but his hand clamped down over her lips. He put mouth to her ear and said something, but she was too terrified to understand it.

She was in a fight for her life.

They lurched around the room together, her feet dangling twelve inches above the floor. Writhing, twisting, she jabbed her elbow into his belly. Nothing. She tried again. Two jabs this time and though he grunted, his hold on her didn't loosen.

She kicked out, caught the table a glancing blow. A

lamp clattered to the floor but it wouldn't be enough to bring anybody running, not in a place like this.

Another kick. Her heel connected with his shin. With his knee. That wrung another grunt and a hiss of pain from him.

All it got her was the swift tightening of his hard arms around her.

She jerked against that unholy embrace and they banged into the iron frame of the bed.

"Goddammit," the man growled, and just the sound of that one word sent her terror into overdrive.

His accent was North American. That meant there was no chance he was a local thief.

He was the man sent to kill her.

Mia caught the heel of his hand between her teeth and bit.

The man cursed. She bit him again, tasted blood, and he put his knee at the base of her spine, pulled her back against him so that her body arched. He spread his hand over both her nose and her mouth.

"Stop it! I'm not going to hurt you."

No. He wasn't going to hurt her. That was why he'd followed her from Cartagena, broken into her room, hidden behind the door and jumped her. Why his moves were those of a professional killer.

If he'd thought his assurance would make her docile, he was wrong. Her struggles grew more frantic.

His hand came down harder. The room started to gray.

She clamped her hands around his arm. Struggled for one last breath.

His hand lifted and she gulped a few precious breaths before he cut off her air again.

"Your choice, baby," he said, his mouth at her ear.

"You want to live or you want to die? Either way, I can accommodate you."

He was lying. She'd die, no matter what, once he'd finished with her. Still, if she played along, she could buy some time.

Mia nodded.

"Smart girl," he said, and let go.

She collapsed like a marionette severed from its strings, slid to the floor and let her head fall back against the wall. Breathing was all that mattered. After a while, when she'd stopped gasping, she looked up at the man who'd been sent to find her.

He'd moved to the window where he stood, arms folded, legs spread apart. Morning sunlight shone in her eyes. She couldn't see him very well. All she knew was that he was big and strong.

Much bigger, much stronger than she was.

"You okay?"

Was she okay? She wanted to laugh, considering that he'd almost killed her. Except, he hadn't. She was no use to anybody, dead. She had to remember that. He'd do whatever it took to control her, to keep her alive until he delivered her to his employer.

She didn't answer. He studied her for a few seconds. Then he went to the cracked sink in the corner, filled a glass with water and brought it to her.

"Drink this."

She wanted to tell him what he could do with the glass but defying him instead of helping herself would have been stupid. She took the glass and drained it, then held it out to him.

She'd play at being passive. Maybe that would give her an edge.

His fingers brushed hers as he took the glass. His skin was warm. Almost hot to the touch. She was freezing but then, that was what happened when you came down from an adrenaline high. And all she was wearing was a thin cotton robe.

Did he know that? Probably, considering how tightly he'd been holding her.

Mia shuddered and pulled the robe more closely around her. He'd be capable of anything. Anything.

"So," he said, his tone soft and almost lazy, "you want to tell me about it?"

She looked up. He was at the window again, still limned in light.

"About what?"

"Come on, Mia. Let's not waste time playing games. Why'd you fake your own abduction?"

"Fake my own…" She shook her head. "I don't know what you're talking about."

"Your boyfriend's upset."

Douglas. Yes. She'd be surprised if he wasn't.

"He thought something had happened to you and all the time, what happened was that you decided to run out on him. The only question now is, where is it?"

Her heart bumped into her throat. She forced herself not to react with any kind of body language.

"Mia. Playing dumb isn't going to help. I asked you a question. Where is it?"

"I'm not playing anything. I don't understand the question." Carefully, not wanting to do anything that might make him come at her again, she sat a little straighter.

"It'll go easier if you tell me."

Easier? She almost laughed. Once he got the list from her, her usefulness to him would be over.

"I told you," she said carefully. "I don't know what you're talking about."

He stepped away from the window and came toward her. God, he was so big! Six-three, six-four. And she was down here, huddled on the floor. She had to even the odds, at least psychologically. Passive was one thing. Submissive was another.

Slowly, her eyes locked to his still-shadowy figure, she rose to her feet.

"I have to get dressed."

His gaze flickered over her, lingering on the thrust of her breasts. She decided to sound a little more assertive.

"Did you hear me? I want to get dressed. I'm cold."

"This is Colombia. We're practically sitting on the equator. It's never cold here."

There was no point in telling him he was wrong. She had the feeling he knew it, that he was trying to bait her. Instead she drew the edges of the robe together.

"I just took a shower. The water was cold and the towels were thin, and I'm—"

"Wet," he said.

His voice had changed. Gone lower. Rougher. Her breath caught. Mentioning the shower had been a bad idea. She could tell by the way he sounded, the way his gaze moved over her.

She glanced down, saw the clear thrust of her nipples beneath the robe. Fear skittered down her spine. She had to defuse things. Personalize the enemy. Wasn't that one of the things you were supposed to do? Her training had been brutally short, but she'd learned some things, at least.

"You didn't…you didn't tell me your name."

"Does it matter?"

"Yes. It matters." Forget submissive. Forget passive.

You met force with force, just as she had when he'd jumped her. Mia tossed back her wet hair. "You break into my room, go through my things, accuse me of—of who knows what—"

"And you," he said softly, "don't even ask why. Interesting, don't you think?"

She could see him clearly now. He was lean. Hard-bodied. His shoulders, encased in a navy cotton T-shirt, were broad. His belly was washboard-flat. His hips were narrow, his legs long in the confines of softly faded jeans.

He had the kind of body that graced ads for high-powered, expensive cars.

Her eyes lifted to his face. It was hard not to react. She'd expected a monster. Instead she saw masculine beauty. Thick black hair. Deep green eyes. A long, elegant blade of a nose. A chiseled mouth, a lightly clefted chin.

She suppressed a bubble of hysterical laughter. No ugly hired assassin for her. She rated the kind of man who could break hearts as well as necks.

She had to come up with an idea, and fast.

"You really had Hamilton fooled."

Mia raised her eyebrows. "Who?"

"What did I tell you, baby? Don't play dumb. It just ticks me off." A smile lifted the corners of his mouth. "But you didn't fool me. I figured you, right from the start. You skipped out with a little something to sweeten the trip."

Her heartbeat stumbled again. She'd been so careful, copying the list. Putting the original back where she'd found it. Maybe he didn't know. Maybe he was fishing.

"You're wrong," she said, her voice so calm it amazed her. "I didn't take anything. I—I left Douglas because—because he—he wouldn't let me break things off."

"Ah. Suddenly you know who old Dougie is."

"Did you expect me to admit it right away? You broke into my room, you attacked me—"

"Mia, Mia, what am I going to do with you? You're lying. If you'd ditched your boyfriend, you'd be in the States by now. You'd have taken the first plane home."

Think, she told herself frantically. Think.

"He'd have had them watch the airports."

"He's a colonel. He isn't God."

She almost laughed. "Try telling that to him."

"To tell you the truth, Mia, I don't give a damn about your feelings for the man. I want what you stole. You going to tell me where it is?"

"Where what is?" she said calmly.

His eyes went flat. "Fine. We'll do it the hard way. Get dressed. And be quick about it. I want to get this over with."

She didn't. As soon as they were alone somewhere…

"Well? I don't have all day."

She stepped away from the door. "I'll get dressed. You wait outside."

His smile curved his mouth again. "Nice try, baby, but it won't work."

She felt heat rise in her face. "I'm not getting dressed with you here."

"Yeah," he said, his voice taking on that roughness again, "you are."

He reached for her. She jerked back but the wall was behind her. Eyes locked to hers, he reached for the sash of her robe. She slapped at him. He grabbed her wrists, tugged her arms high over her head with one hand and undid the sash with the other.

Any second, she was going to scream.

Matthew knew it. The woman was like a wildcat, fighting, struggling, refusing to admit she was caught.

"You make a sound," he growled, "you'll regret it."

"Let go. Let—go! Damn you, let—"

He silenced her the only way he could.

With his mouth.

She cried out against his lips, tried to twist away from him. He moved closer, tightened his grip on her wrists and kissed her harder.

She was frantic now, whimpering into his mouth, her heart racing against his. She was terrified and she damned well should be, pulling a stunt that had driven Hamilton half-crazy, stealing dope, driving into these bandit-infested hills.

She was the kind of woman who did whatever she pleased and to hell with morality, who used her looks to get what she wanted.

How could she taste like heaven?

Reality blurred. He captured both her wrists in one hand. Cupped her face with the other. Changed the angle of the kiss. Nipped at her bottom lip and when she cried out at the tiny pain, he used the moment to slip his tongue into her mouth.

She gasped. Struggled.

And then—and then, she made the faintest whisper of sound.

The sound a woman makes when she gives herself to a man.

Matthew let go of her wrists and thrust his hands into her hair. He tilted her face up to his and he took the kiss deeper, deeper, deeper…

Mia exploded into action. Beat at him with her fists. Raised her knee, aimed for his most vulnerable spot and would have done damage if he hadn't reacted quickly, grabbed her hands, pinned them to the wall and pinned her body to it, too, with the weight of his.

They stared at each other for a long minute, both breathing hard. Then, slowly, still holding her hands, Matthew took a step back.

Her robe had opened during the struggle.

He dropped his eyes to see what he'd uncovered.

High, creamy breasts with pale pink nipples. A taut navel. A delicate blur of dark, silky curls.

He fought not to let anything show in his face, though she'd have been blind not to see that he was hard as stone, his erection straining for release against his fly.

He thought of taking her. Here. Right here, against the wall. No matter how she'd try to deny it, she'd felt the same swift rush of desire. He'd tasted it in her kiss, heard it in her whispered response. Could still see it now, in her passion-blurred eyes. In the taut budding of her nipples.

All he had to do was unzip his jeans, cup her bottom, lift her onto the urgency of his straining, swollen flesh. If she protested, it would last only seconds, only until she took all of him deep inside, until he thrust into her, until she gave a high, keening cry and came...

Sweet Jesus, had he lost his mind?

This was a job. A job he hadn't wanted. She was running dope or she'd stolen it from whoever supplied her, and he'd spent years of his life hating people like her.

On top of all that, she was another man's woman. She could say what she wanted about Hamilton but that didn't change the fact that she belonged to the man.

The hell with her little moans. A woman could fake that. This one could, and did, all the time.

It was probably how she'd worked Hamilton.

Matthew's eyes darkened with distaste. For himself, and for the all-but-naked woman in front of him.

"Is this how you kept poor Dougie blind to what you were doing?" he said coldly. "Letting him think you'd let him have this someday?"

"I don't know what you—"

Mia's breath caught. His hand was at her breast, the tips of his fingers feathering across the nipple. She wasn't a virgin. A man had caressed her breasts before but it had never made her feel   made her feel—

Terror flooded her senses.

Terror, and something else, something infinitely darker.

"I couldn't figure it out. How such a smart guy could be such a sucker." Matthew smiled thinly. "Then I saw his house. The sleeping arrangements. And I thought, the man's an idiot, letting her sleep by herself." He dipped his head, inhaled the soft, white-floral scent of her hair. "Now it's starting to make sense. You teased him the way a mare teases a stud, giving him hints at what he could have if he behaved himself."

"You're crazy! I never—"

She caught her breath as he cupped her breast. His palm felt rough; when he ran his thumb over her nipple she jerked back…

And felt a tug of liquid heat low in her belly.

The cold, she thought frantically, that's what it was. That's what it had to be. The cold and her fear.

"The thing is, Dougie didn't know how to handle you." A smile angled across her captor's hard mouth. "But I do."

Suddenly he stepped back. Mia swayed, clutched the lapels of the robe, fought to keep her legs from buckling.

"Get dressed. Do it fast, or I'll do it for you."

Looking into his eyes was like looking into a glacier.
No softness, no sentiment, nothing but unremitting force.

He walked to the chair and sat down. Folded his
arms. Crossed his feet at the ankles.

She noticed, as if it mattered, that he was wearing
scuffed Western boots.

Mia waited. So did he.

Finally Mia turned her back and let the robe slip
from her shoulders.

CHAPTER THREE

THE ROBE slid down her arms, slowly revealing her back, and stopped at the base of her spine.

Even from this angle, Matthew could see that she was beautiful.

Her skin was a pale gold; her hair a fall of deepest chocolate touched with auburn by the light streaming through the window.

She might have been a painting by Monet or Renoir. *Woman Getting Dressed.* A canvas people would stare at on the wall of a famous museum, seeing not so much the brushstrokes and the talent of the painter but the beauty of the woman herself.

She had a small birthmark on one shoulder and another an inch or two lower. He could put his mouth to the first, kiss his way to the next.

Kiss his way down her spine to the delicate indentation at its base. How would it taste, if he put the tip of his tongue there?

What would she do if he went to her, cupped her shoulders, put his lips to her throat? Would she lean back against him? Close her eyes with pleasure as he lowered the robe, bared her buttocks, then drew her against him so she could feel the heaviness of his erection pressing against her?

Hell!

He wasn't a voyeur. Undressing a woman was a man's pleasure. So was watching a woman's face as she undressed for him.

This was business. He had no choice but to watch her...

Matthew dragged a shuddering breath into his lungs.

Who was he kidding? Watching her was turning him on. How long was it since he'd had a woman? Too long, obviously, otherwise—otherwise—

She reached for something on the bed. The forward motion made her body arch. Tilted her bottom toward him.

Ah, God, he was going to turn to stone! But he had to watch her. He hadn't done a thorough search. For all he knew, she had a weapon stashed.

Okay. She'd found whatever she'd been looking for.

She straightened, then stood on one foot. She was putting on her panties with the robe as a screen.

Clever.

Not so clever, a sly voice murmured. No matter what she did, she'd have to drop the robe eventually.

He folded his arms. His gaze moved over her again.

It was pointless to pretend he didn't enjoy watching her. She was a woman born to excite a man. Even now, he could close his eyes and see her face and its perfection of innocence. Her rounded breasts. The smooth skin that led to the exquisite whorl of dark curls he'd glimpsed before.

No wonder Hamilton had been taken in. He almost felt sorry for the man. Who could stand up to witchery like this?

She had gone absolutely still. There was tension in

every line of her body. Yeah. There would be, he thought, shifting his weight in the chair.

It was moment of truth time.

She had to let go of the robe in order to finish dressing.

"Won't you at least turn your back?"

"No," he said coolly. "I won't."

She muttered something he couldn't catch. Matthew suppressed a grin. He had to give her credit. She had balls.

A couple of seconds went by and then she let the robe fall to the floor.

His mouth went dry.

She'd put on a pair of those plain white cotton panties.

The women he knew wore silk or lace. He liked that. The sensual glide of a soft fabric. The flirtatiousness of lace. He liked black and scarlet, colors that contrasted with the delicacy of skin.

Cotton was for T-shirts and gym shorts and—and how in hell could those white cotton panties look so sexy?

Was it the starkness of them against her golden skin? Or the very simplicity of them, the realization that what they hid from his eyes were the sweetest secrets of her body?

What would happen if he came up behind her? Bent his head, sank his teeth lightly into her shoulder while he slid his hand into that plain white cotton and cupped the gentle swell of her backside, moved his fingers over her flesh until they reached the delicate petals that guarded her womanhood.

Holy hell. He kept this up, he was in trouble.

She took something from the bed. A bra. Slipped it on and closed it. Good. He could breathe again. Next, she'd put on the T-shirt…

Instead she reached her hands to the cups and though he couldn't see what she was doing, he could imagine it.

She was doing that little thing women did. Cupping her own breasts. Arranging them in the bra. Touching the silken skin he ached to touch, to taste…

He shot to his feet. "Hurry it up," he said coldly. "Pack the rest of your stuff and do it pronto."

She pulled on a pair of white cotton trousers. Yanked a pale gray T-shirt over her head. Slid her feet into her shoes and turned toward him, fully dressed right down to sandals that showed ten delicate pink toenails.

He had to clench his jaw to keep from going to her and tossing her down on the bed.

It was the situation, that's what it was. Danger, risk, the unknown. Add a good-looking woman, stir well and you ended up with a lot of heat.

Some color had come back to her face. Getting some clothes on did that for prisoners. He didn't want that. He wanted her scared. She'd be easier to handle and quicker to tell him what he wanted to know.

"Come here."

She gestured at the suitcase. "But you said—"

"I know what I said. Come here."

She moved toward him slowly, her eyes locked to his face. Such enormous eyes. They were the color of rich coffee, though when the light caught them a certain way, he could see flecks of green and gold in the irises.

"Put your palms flat against the wall and step back."

The color faded from her cheeks. "What?"

"You have a hearing problem? Put your hands against the wall and step back."

Her mouth began to tremble. For a couple of seconds, he almost told her to forget it. He'd seen her naked; he knew damned well she didn't have a gun...

But this wasn't about guns, it was about control.

"Do it," he snarled.

She swung away from him. Pressed her palms to the wall. Stepped back...and, of course, had to spread her legs to keep her balance.

He moved in. Reached around her. Cupped her breasts. He made sure his touch was impersonal. Still, she jumped as if he'd touched her with a hot iron.

"Stand still."

"No!" She swung toward him, eyes glittering with hatred. "You can't do this. You don't have the right."

"Correction, baby. I have *all* the right."

"The hell you do."

Matthew smiled. Drew his gun from the small of his back. Watched her eyes widen when she saw it.

"This gives me whatever right I need. Now turn around and get your hands on that wall."

"You're a pig," she said, her voice shaking with contempt.

"Now, that really breaks my heart," he said, and spun her away from him.

He moved his hands over her quickly, expertly, checking her belly, her legs down all the way to her ankles, then coming up again and touching the insides of her thighs.

He hesitated. Then he put his hand between her legs and cupped her.

She made a little sound of despair. He imagined how he could change it to a whisper of desire. All he had to do was move his hand. Stroke her. She hated him, yes, but memory of that kiss told him she'd damned well respond to him, just the same.

She'd be a thousand times easier to handle, if he made love to her.

Matthew shut his eyes.

One of the reasons he'd left the Agency was because he'd known he was losing the ability to separate what was morally right from what was practical and expedient. Could twenty-four hours in his old life turn him into that kind of man again?

No. It couldn't. This was right, and it was expedient. Mia Palmieri was running drugs. Whatever it took to stop her, he would do.

He took a step back. "Okay," he said briskly, "turn around."

She swung toward him, her eyes as hard and cold as amber. Good. From now on, she'd behave. All he had to do was decide what to do with her.

It was, he thought glumly, a damned good question.

Hamilton had only asked him to find out what had happened to her. Well, he'd found out. She'd run away. In theory, he could just let her keep running.

But not if she had a stash of uncut cocaine. He'd put in too much time and sweat stopping drug runners to let that happen. Alita had died, to keep it from happening.

Letting Mia Palmieri go wasn't an option, not if she was on the run with dope.

If he found the stuff…well, that would give him other options. He could flush it down a toilet and let her walk away. He wasn't a cop; he wasn't even a spook anymore. He had no obligation to bring her to justice.

If she was running from the cartel…what then? Same deal as before. Take away the drugs and give her a running start. The cartel people would find her eventually, but that wasn't his problem.

She was Hamilton's problem. Hamilton's woman.

Why did that make his belly knot?

Matthew scowled. First things first. If she was carrying dope, he'd find it. Then he could decide what to do next.

"You done packing?"

Her suitcase closed with a snap. "Yes."

"Listen closely, because I don't want any mistakes. I'm going to open the door. We're going down the stairs together, me with my arm around you. We're going to look like the happiest lovers since Romeo and Juliet."

"Where are we going?"

"Wherever I say."

She shot him a look that said she hoped he'd burn in hell.

"You sure you haven't forgotten anything?"

She nodded. "I'm sure."

"Because if you have, consider it gone."

"I told you, I haven't forgotten anything."

Fine. The dope wasn't in the room. Nobody, no matter how scared, left a stash worth big bucks behind.

He clasped her wrist. She tried to shake free and he wrapped his arm around her shoulders.

"Lovers, remember? Romeo and Juliet."

Her teeth glittered in a parody of a smile. "Romeo died."

The quick retort would be to remind her that Juliet died, too. He didn't say it. For some reason, the quip was too filled with foreboding. Despite his Comanche blood, he wasn't in to predicting the future, but had a bad feeling as he unlocked the door and stepped out into the corridor.

One arm at her waist, the other within easy reach of his gun, he took her down the stairs, out the door and to the street. There was a café across the way.

"Breakfast," he said.

She looked at him as if he were crazy. Maybe he was, but if he didn't get some food in his belly soon, he'd fall on his face.

The café smelled like the grease on the griddle was a permanent fixture, but how bad could coffee, eggs and sausage be?

Pretty bad, as it turned out. After a couple of bites, Matthew pushed his plate away. Mia hadn't ordered anything except coffee and he figured she'd made the smartest choice.

Over his second cup, he leaned over the scarred table.

"Have you come to your senses?"

"About what?"

"About coming across with what you stole."

"I told you, I don't know what you're talking about."

"Don't be stupid," he said sharply. "Think about what will happen if you don't come clean with me."

Her cheeks paled but she didn't answer. He took some bills from his pocket, dumped them on the table and got to his feet.

"Let's go," he muttered.

He grabbed her arm and the suitcase and led her across the street to her car.

"Open it."

"Whatever you're looking for…I don't have it. No matter what you do to me—"

"Open the damned car."

She dug the keys from her purse, opened the door and he pushed her inside. "Sit," he commanded. When she complied, he took the keys from her, got behind the wheel and burned rubber getting out of the lot.

Twenty minutes later, he found the kind of place he needed, a turnoff that led through some trees to a small lake. There were empty beer bottles strewn around but it looked as if nobody had been there in a long time.

"Get out."

She didn't move. He tugged her out of the car and yanked off his belt. Her eyes welled with tears. She began to tremble. He expected her to beg but she didn't.

She was ballsy, all right. He had to give her that.

Matthew wrapped the belt around her wrists and dragged her over to a tree.

"Think about what you're doing," she said. "Killing me won't solve anything."

He looked at her, his eyebrows raised in surprise. She was serious. Who did she think he was? Some goon from the cartel, even though he'd told her Hamilton had sent him?

He could tell her the truth. That he wasn't involved with the cartel and he certainly wasn't going to kill her...but if that's what she thought, let her. Her fear would make her malleable.

"I'll do whatever I have to do," he said coldly. And then, because the look in her eyes reminded him all too clearly of the life he'd once led, he cursed, went to her and dropped a hard, lingering kiss on her mouth.

Her soft mouth, trembling now with fear and damp with tears.

Desire flashed through him, hot as a poker and just as sharp. Matthew cursed again, stepped back and used the belt to secure her to the tree.

"Behave yourself," he said sharply. "If you do,

you'll come through this okay. One last time, then. Where is it?"

She didn't answer. He shook his head, went to the car and began systematically taking it apart. The obvious places first: glove box, console, the trunk.

Nothing.

The seat cushions were next. He slit them open with his pocketknife. Then he slashed the spare tire, tossed everything out of the trunk.

Still nothing.

There were other places to hide drugs. Inside the door panels. In secret compartments under the floor. But this was a rental vehicle. There wouldn't be any secret compartments, and she hadn't had time to get inside the door panels.

Matthew put his hands on his hips and gave the torn-up vehicle a long, appraising stare. He dumped everything back into the trunk. Then he walked to where he'd left Mia. He had to shake her up, but how?

Prison. A Colombian prison. You wouldn't kennel a stray dog in those that he'd seen. Would she know that? Yes. He'd bet she would.

"Okay," he said matter-of-factly, "that's it. I've done what I can. You leave me no choice. I'll have to take you back."

"Back?" Her face paled. "To Hamilton?"

It wasn't the answer he'd expected but the look in her eyes told him to go with it.

"Sure. He's the guy who asked me to find you."

"No," she said in a low voice. "Please. Don't do that." She lifted her head and her eyes met his. "I don't know who you are," she whispered, "or what you think I've done but I beg you, don't send me back to him."

She sounded terrified. Matthew told himself it didn't mean a damn. She was one fine actress, that was all. Look how she'd fooled her own lover.

"You don't want me to send you back? Fine. Just tell me where the dope is."

"The what?"

"Come on, baby. The cocaine. Tell me where you hid it and I'll let you go. What happens between you and the colonel is your business. The dope is mine."

"I don't have drugs! Thinking I do is crazy. You searched my room. Searched my car." Two stripes of crimson angled along her cheeks. "You even searched me. If I had cocaine, you'd have found it."

She was right, he thought. He would have.

"Then, why did you run?"

"I told you. Douglas wouldn't let me end our relationship."

"Right," Matthew said coldly. "So, what was he going to do? Lock you in your room and throw away the key?" She turned her face away and he caught her chin, jerked her head toward him. "You had old Dougie by the balls. Separate rooms, no sex… I'm right, aren't I? There wasn't any sex."

"I—I—"

"Answer the question, damn it. Were you sleeping with him?"

The world, and time, seemed to stop. Her eyes met his and he waited, waited…

"Of course I slept with him," she said. "He was my fiancé. Why wouldn't I?"

Why wouldn't she, indeed?

"Yeah." Matthew cleared his throat. "Yeah," he said

again, and his voice roughened. "I guess teasing the poor bastard could only take you so far."

"Does insulting a woman make you feel good?"

He had to give her credit. She was terrified, but she was determined to give as good as she got.

"I want to know why you ran away."

"I told you. Douglas wouldn't—"

"That's bull," he said bluntly. "You ran because you took something that wasn't yours."

"I didn't take anything," she said, but she was lying. He saw it in the sudden contraction of her pupils and all at once, he knew he'd been lured into a game where the only rule was survival.

Working quickly, he untied her and hustled her to the car. He shoved her inside, got behind the wheel and started the engine. The car lurched forward.

He ditched it a couple of hundred yards from the inn. Whoever found it in this godforsaken town would undoubtedly view it as a gift from the gods. The car would never be seen again.

"What are you doing?" Mia demanded as he bundled her into his SUV. "Who are you? What do you want from me?"

"A couple of minutes of silence, for a start."

"No! Answer my questions. Tell me who you are and what you want."

Involuntarily his eyes went from her face to her breasts. Her face colored and he knew she was remembering what had happened in the hotel room.

Hell, so was he.

"Try to get this straight," he said coldly. "I ask the questions. You give the answers. That's it."

"I have the right to know your na—"

She cried out as he clasped her shoulders and pulled her to him.

"You have no rights, baby. The only thing you need to know is that I'm going to find out why you ran. What you stole. Where you're go—"

His cell phone rang.

The sound surprised him. His brothers knew he was out of the country; they'd be unlikely to call him, and few other people had the number.

He let go of Mia. She shrank back against the seat as he took the phone from his pocket and flipped open the cover.

"Yes?"

"Mr. Knight."

It was the colonel. *How will I get in touch with you?* he'd said, and Matthew had rattled off the cell number.

"Yes?"

"I was hoping you'd made progress in your search for my fiancée."

Matthew looked at Mia. Her eyes glittered as much with defiance as with fear.

One word to Hamilton, and this would be over. He didn't even have to return to Cartagena. The colonel could easily arrange to have someone meet him here to pick her up.

"Mr. Knight? Do we have a bad connection? I asked if you'd made progress."

"I heard you, Colonel."

"Well, have you? Have you found Mia yet?"

Matthew looked at the woman beside him again.

"No," he said calmly, "I haven't."

He closed the phone, tucked it back into his pocket and started the Escalade's engine. Then, in what was perhaps the most illogical act of his life, he leaned across the console and took her mouth in a quick, hard kiss.

Moments later, the inn and the town were far behind them, lost in a cloud of leaves and dust.

CHAPTER FOUR

THE MAN sent to find her drove like a madman.

But then, why wouldn't he? Weren't killers nutcases by definition? And that's what he was. A killer. "Finding" her was just a sorry attempt to hide from the truth.

Mia risked a glance at him.

She'd met killers before. There'd been men who'd come to Hamilton's villa late at night. None had come right out and said, "Hello, I'm on the cartel's payroll as a hired gun," but she knew what they were.

Most of them looked as if taking a life would be no more trouble than swatting a fly.

Not her captor.

He was good-looking. Actually, that was an understatement. He was heart-stoppingly beautiful and yet completely masculine. He reminded her of the statue of David she'd seen on that trip to Florence, her senior year in college…

Or of a big, exotic cat.

And that was exactly what he was. A powerful, magnificent, predator. He'd wasted no time proving it to her, either. The way he'd treated her… Making her stand naked before him. Watching her dress. Putting his hands on her.

His hands.

An electric tingle shot through her body.

What a horrible thing to have done. Touching her so intimately. Caressing her nipples. Pretending he was searching her and cupping her breasts. Touching her between her thighs.

She shuddered.

She'd hated it. Hated him…

Hated herself for responding. For wanting to moan as much as she'd wanted to weep. For wanting to close her eyes. Lean back. Feel his hard body supporting hers. Turn in his arms, seek his mouth…

Mia swung away and stared blindly out the window.

She knew why he'd done it. It was all about power. Domination. Making it clear that he was in charge. She even knew…she shut her eyes, then opened them again. She even knew why she'd had those insane reactions when he touched her.

In situations as highly charged as this, fear could give way to something darker. A bond, between captor and captive.

It could benefit him by making her compliant.

Or it could benefit her.

Unless she'd read him wrong, he was attracted to her. She swallowed dryly. False modesty was stupid at a time like this. He was more than attracted.

He wanted her.

Maybe sex and violence were all part of the same thing in his head.

Knowing that, understanding it, could give *her* power. She could use his desire. Work him. Finesse him. God help her, seduce him, if she had to.

And the probability was that she'd have to because if he took her back to Cartagena…

If he did, she was as good as dead.

Hamilton would have her killed. What she'd suspected about him had made her dangerous. What she'd found and taken before she left, marked her for removal.

At least she had some kind of a chance with this man.

Mia cleared her throat, then looked at him.

"You're wrong, you know."

He glanced at her. Was that amusement in his eyes?

"Really."

She nodded. "You know my name. I should know yours."

"Meaning, I've forgotten my manners?" His tone mocked her. Then, to her surprise, he nodded. "Why not? I'm Matthew. Matthew Knight."

"And you work for…?"

"I don't work for anybody."

"You're a private contractor."

Something in the way she phrased the statement made Matthew wary. It was a strange choice of words.

"You might say that I'm here as a favor to your boyfriend."

"He isn't my boyfriend."

"Sorry. Your fiancé."

She started to tell him he was wrong on that, too, but why bother? Matthew Knight would go on thinking whatever he liked.

"I thought you might be Colombian. You speak Spanish like a native."

"Don't waste your time trying to flatter me."

"It was just a comment."

She waited, but he was silent. After a while, she tried again.

"Are you North American?"

"Last time I checked, Dallas was in North America."

"How do you know Douglas?"

"Through a mutual acquaintance."

Her determination to play cool and calm evaporated. "Damn it, don't you ever say anything that has meaning?"

Matthew looked at her. "The sky is very blue today," he said politely. "Not a cloud in sight."

She wanted to hit him. Just ball up her fist and let fly.

"At least tell me where you're taking me."

"I told you. Somewhere quiet, where we can talk."

A cave? A shack in the mountains? A place where nobody could hear her scream?

She took a deep breath. "If you let me go—" She swallowed dryly as he downshifted into a tight turn. "If you let me go, nobody has to know about it."

"I'd know. So would your boyfriend."

"I told you, he isn't my boyfriend."

"Try telling him that."

"Besides, he wouldn't know. I certainly wouldn't tell him. Neither would you."

"And what would you give me, if I did let you go?"

Her heartbeat quickened. "What would you want?"

"I don't know, baby." His voice turned husky. "You're the one making the offer."

She could offer herself to him. Wasn't that what she'd just been thinking?

No. She couldn't do it.

Mia took an unsteady breath.

But—but sleeping with him would be incredibly exciting. He wouldn't hurt her. Not in bed. Crazy as it was, she knew that. What he'd do, what he'd make her feel, might be dangerous, but only in ways her suddenly thickening blood told her she'd find pleasurable.

And he'd be in command. Of her. Of himself. Even when he'd searched her, she'd been aware of his sense of control. What would it be like to make him lose that control? To make him forget himself in her arms?

"Well? I'm waiting."

Mia touched the tip of her tongue to her suddenly dry lips. "I could—I could pay you."

He grinned. "Now, there's a thought. How much?"

"How much do you want?"

"Oh, I don't know. Let me think. How does a billion dollars sound?"

He laughed. Mia felt her cheeks flush.

"You think this is amusing."

"You can't buy me off, Mia. Don't waste your time trying."

He wasn't stupid. She had to remember that, just as she had to remember that he was only muscle for hire and she was a trained agent.

A semi-trained agent, she thought, and swallowed a hysterical laugh.

"You could tell Douglas that I escaped."

"From me?"

That won her an incredulous stare. The arrogance of the man!

"Yes," Mia said. "From you."

"Nobody would believe it."

A hill rose ahead of them, cutting through trees that looked as if they'd stood here for hundreds of years. Matthew eased the swift-moving Escalade around a tight turn and suddenly a valley opened before them.

Towering trees. Lush ferns. A lazy ribbon of sapphire-blue. And a house. Big. Sprawling. A house that seemed to be all glass.

"Is this it? The place you're taking me?"

No answer. She felt a tightening in her throat.

"Is it?"

"Just sit back and relax."

"But—but where are we?"

"Where nobody will bother us," he said in a flat voice and Mia realized, in that instant, that the old cliché was true.

Your blood *could* run cold.

The road into the valley had not changed.

Narrow. Winding. A dizzying drop on one side and a wall of green on the other. Matthew had loved this place on sight when he first saw it, all those years ago. He'd spent a long weekend here, courtesy of some fat-cat Department of Defense official who'd owned it.

"My wife's Colombian. She inherited the place from her uncle," the guy had said, "but I'm gonna unload it. Damned thing isn't worth keeping, out in the freaking middle of nowhere."

The fact that it was in the freaking middle of nowhere was what had appealed to Matthew. A determined enemy could find you virtually anywhere, but this terrain made the job ten times more difficult.

And then there was the primitive beauty of the quiet forest, the swift rush of the river and the idyllic pool hidden in a clearing he thought might never have known a human footprint until his.

Back home, the Agency just a bad memory, money

piling in from his new business, he'd phoned the guy from DOD, asked if he was still interested in selling.

He was, and he'd named a price that seemed right. Actually, any price would have seemed right back then. Matthew was still awakening in the middle of the night with images of Alita's violated body burning his brain.

Somehow or other, he'd thought going to the house that was now his, giving himself over to a place where time and evil had no meaning, would dispel his demons. He'd never found out if that were true.

Returning to Colombia had begun to look about as reasonable as returning to a nightmare.

Now, the valley seemed the only safe place.

Something was wrong with this entire setup. Nobody had told him the truth. You got used to that, when you were in Cloak and Dagger Land, but he wasn't on that turf anymore.

The colonel had asked him to find his fiancée.

Simple enough, or so it had seemed. But the colonel's fiancée kept insisting she wasn't his fiancée, and the colonel seemed less concerned with what might have happened to the woman he supposedly loved than he was with locating her.

Wouldn't her welfare be paramount? This was a big country. Most of it was beautiful, but parts of it were more dangerous than Mogadishu at midnight.

How come the colonel had never once expressed concern over Mia being out there, alone?

Then there was Mia. How come she'd tried to smuggle dope? How come she was on the run? If the answer was cocaine, Matthew would have found it by now.

And, finally, the million dollar question.

How come all he could think about was getting Mia Palmieri naked on a bed?

Matthew brought the SUV to a stop outside the triple doors of the garage. He took the keys from the ignition, found the one for the front door and got out from behind the wheel.

"End of the line," he said. "Everybody out."

Mia didn't even blink. She sat, motionless, hands knotted in her lap, eyes straight ahead. Was every step going to be a battle?

He went around the truck and opened her door.

"Here's the deal. You get out and walk, or I pull you out and toss you over my shoulder. Since I'm tired and hungry and generally pissed off, I'm probably not going to be particularly gentle about it but hey, the decision is yours."

He almost laughed at the look she gave him, but she wasn't stupid. She undid her seat belt and started to step down.

Matthew caught her in his arms.

"Wouldn't want you to hurt yourself," he said with a hard smile.

"Thank you so much for your concern."

Her words were like little bee stings, sharp and meant to hurt, but he was coming to expect that kind of toughness from her. The further she got, mentally, from the shock of finding him in her room in that sleazy hotel, the stronger she became.

He'd have to change that.

Wasn't it a good thing he'd discovered the way to do it? he thought, and he gathered her against him and kissed her.

It wasn't the kind of kiss a man gives a woman who stirs his heart; it was the kind a man gives a woman he wants to dominate. Matthew held nothing back. Mouth, teeth, tongue... his kiss was savage.

Mia reacted, as he'd intended, with fear. She twisted in his arms, pounded her fists against his shoulders, but he was relentless, holding her so tightly against him that her struggles only brought her breasts and hips in closer contact with his body.

Somehow, she managed to free her mouth long enough to gasp for air and then call him a name he'd rarely heard a woman use.

The oath was still on her lips when he crushed her mouth beneath his again. When he ended the kiss, it was only so he could cup her face, tilt it to him, look into those dark brown eyes and see what he wanted there, her despair and her capitulation.

What he saw in her eyes were the tears of a frightened woman.

Good, he thought savagely. That was the way he wanted her. Scared. Helpless. Ready to tell him everything he needed to know…

And then he stopped thinking and kissed her again. Gently. Softly…

In a heartbeat, everything changed.

Mia began to tremble, but in a way he understood. She clasped his shoulders and rose toward him, her lips yielding to the light pressure of his. She made that sound, the one that had almost driven him to his knees the last time, and let him inside the velvet warmth of her mouth.

And he was lost.

Lost in her heat. Her sweetness. In the feeling that they were alone on the planet, that nothing mattered but this. Nothing but this. This…

Matthew tore his mouth from hers.

Jesus, what was he doing?

He clasped her shoulders. Pushed her away, his breathing as ragged as if he'd run a mile, and let fly with the rage he felt at her for trying to seduce him, at himself for being such a damned easy mark.

"You keep offering," he said, his voice low and flat, "and, sooner or later, baby, I'm going to accept." Her face whitened and he caught her chin and forced her head up until her eyes met his. "You're playing with fire, little girl. If you get burned, don't blame me."

Mia followed her captor into the house as obediently as a leashed dog.

Not that she had a choice.

He had a grip on her wrist that would have made her cry out, except she'd be damned if she'd give him the satisfaction.

He was on to her. Evidently she wasn't as good at seducing a man as she'd hoped. One kiss, and he'd known what she was doing...

And wasn't it a good thing that one of them did?

Because—because the ugly truth was, she'd gone from fighting him to wanting him in a heartbeat. Her reaction hadn't been planned. It had just happened. His mouth had felt so tender. He'd tasted so good. Clean and masculine and—and, okay, if she was going for honesty, even when he'd been forcing his kisses on her, even as she'd fought him....

Even then, she'd wanted him.

She'd felt as if her entire body was on fire, a need and a heat blazing in her belly, in her breasts, that she'd never known before. She'd wanted him to carry her into the house, back her against the wall and take her and take her until she was sobbing his name…

"…coffee?"

She blinked in confusion. She'd only caught the end of whatever he'd said. Had it required an answer?

She moistened her lips. "I didn't—I didn't hear you."

"I said, there's a kitchen down the hall. Do you know how to make coffee, or does your usefulness begin and end in bed?"

For the second time in just a few hours, she wanted to rush at him and gouge runnels in his face, pound him with her fists—but she knew how pointless that would be. He was too big, too powerful, and he'd probably end up laughing at her.

Still, she was grateful for what he'd just said. It was the perfect reminder that her sexual fantasies about this unfeeling son of a bitch were sick.

"Actually, I could use a cup of coffee. Show me where the kitchen is and I'll make some. Then, if you're very lucky, there might be enough left for you."

His mouth twitched. How nice, she thought coldly. She was providing comic relief.

"Down that hall. To the right. The coffee's in the freezer, the sugar's in the cupboard along with a couple of boxes of long-lasting milk."

"Fine. Oh, one last thing." She smiled sweetly. "Where do you keep the rat poison? I'd hate to keep you waiting while I search for it."

His eyes narrowed into green slits. "Keep it up," he said softly. "See just how far you can push before I reach overload."

The thought of him on overload sent a chill down her spine but she kept the phony smile on her lips.

"I'm sure I'll be able to tell before that happens. The smoke rising from your circuit-boards will be a dead giveaway."

It was a good line and she made her exit on it, the spot between her shoulder blades tingling in expectation that he'd come after her, but he didn't. She even thought she heard him laugh, but that had to be a mistake.

She found the kitchen easily enough, a big, bright room loaded with shiny stainless-steel appliances and enough gadgets to satisfy any man's soul. The coffee was where he'd said it would be, as were the sugar and milk.

Whose house was this? she wondered as the coffee dripped slowly through the filter. She went to the sliding glass doors that led out to a large deck surrounded by flowering shrubs in a riot of colors.

A place this beautiful wouldn't belong to a man who was a killer. But that's what Matthew Knight was. He'd brought her here so they could be alone. So he could do whatever he figured it would take to wring the truth from her.

Mia shuddered.

What was she doing, making coffee? He'd left her alone. All that stood between her and freedom was a glass door...

"Don't even think about it."

She whirled around. He was right behind her. How could a man his size move so quietly?

"The doors and windows are all on a security circuit. Touch one and they all lock, and enough sirens go off so that there wouldn't be a chance in hell you could evade me." His smile was quick and sharp. "In other words, you're trapped."

Trapped. The word was terrifying, but she'd be

damned if she'd let him know it. She turned away from him and reached for the coffeepot.

"I'm impressed," she said, as if she actually gave a damn. "A high-tech security systems, all this land... Who owns this place?"

"I do."

Her surprise must have shown on her face.

"Want to see the deed? It's mine, baby. Lock, stock and barrel."

"Don't call me that. And why are we here?"

"I told you. For the peace and—"

"Damn it," Mia said, the words tumbling from her lips without plan, "stop toying with me! Whatever it is you're going to do, just—just do it and get it over with."

The careful mask she'd worn had slipped. Matthew heard fear in her voice and saw it in her eyes. She thought he was going to hurt her unless she came clean.

For one crazy minute, he came close to taking her in his arms and telling her that no matter what she'd done, he wouldn't hurt her. Wouldn't let anyone else hurt her...

But the insanity passed.

She was dealing in drugs.

She was another man's woman.

Nothing about her was any good, except for the feel of her in his arms. The taste of her against his lips.

Just the thought of her in Hamilton's arms, in his bed...

He shut his eyes. Forced himself to take a couple of cleansing breaths.

"We'll talk later," he said. "Right now, I want dinner."

"Talk?" Her voice rose. "Talk? Is that what you want me to believe? That you brought me here to have a nice, civilized conversation?"

He was on her in an instant, dragging her against him,

claiming her mouth with his and savagely slipping his hand under her T-shirt to cup her breast.

"Nothing I feel about you is civilized," he said roughly. "And I don't like it. You got that? I'm fed up with you trying to play me for a fool, Mia. Stop it before you force me to do something about it."

"Don't," she said, her voice high and breathless.

"Don't what?" He shoved his hand under her bra; she gasped as his fingers closed on her nipple. "Don't do this?" His fingers moved, moved again, and she tried to choke back the cry that rose in her throat but he heard it and exulted in it. "I want you, goddammit," he growled. "And you want me."

"No! I don't. I don't!"

He cupped the back of her head, his fingers tangling in her hair, and kissed her without mercy until, at last, she surrendered, to him and to herself, sobbing his name against his mouth.

"Matthew," she whispered, "oh, Matthew…"

It was the first time she'd spoken his name, and the sound of it on her lips echoed in his blood.

Nobody had ever said his name the way she did.

"Again. Say it again." When she didn't, he kissed her, hard, hard enough to taste the warm saltiness of blood. Hers or his, it didn't matter. All that mattered was her scent, her touch, her taste. "Damn you," he growled, "say my name."

"Matthew," she whispered, "Matthew, Matthew…"

She was coming apart in his arms. Kissing him, sucking his tongue into her mouth, her hands up under his shirt, moving on his skin.

He pushed her back against the counter. Grabbed the neckline of her shirt and ripped it to the hem. Then he bent his head, bit lightly at a cotton-covered nipple and when she groaned, he bit it again.

It wasn't enough. He needed the sweet taste of her naked breast. He raised his head, took her mouth with his, fumbled with the clasp of her bra, snarled and tore it in half.

Her breasts were beautiful. Round as apples and the color of richest cream. He wanted to feast his eyes on her but not now. Not now, when he could take a delicate pink nipple in his mouth, suck it, lave it until it glistened.

Ah, the incredible taste of her! She was wildflowers and honey against his tongue.

"You're beautiful," he whispered, cupping her breasts, tonguing one taut bud and then the other before drawing each deep into the heat of his mouth. "I've never wanted a woman as I want you."

She was trembling in his arms. Holding him tight. Moving her hips against his.

He took her hand and brought it to him, flattening it over his erection.

On a soft moan, she cupped the denim that strained across his swollen flesh. For one terrible second, he was afraid he was going to come just from that touch, from that female whimper of desire.

"Matthew," she said desperately, "please…"

Her knees buckled and she collapsed in his embrace. He swung her up into his arms and took her mouth again, biting into her bottom lip, savoring her taste even as slid his hand down her thigh, into that sweet, secret place between her legs.

He tore his mouth from hers and looked into her eyes, clouded with passion.

"Tell me," he said thickly.

Her lips parted but the words he needed to hear didn't come. In some microscopic, still-reasoning part of his brain he understood the reason. She knew this was insane, knew it shouldn't be happening...

"Tell me," he demanded.

A tremor went through her. She put her hand against his cheek. "Please," she whispered, "Matthew, please... Take me to bed."

Pure male triumph filled his veins. He started from the room and Mia looped her hands behind his neck. She tried to bury her hot face in his shoulder but he wouldn't let her.

He kissed her instead, kissed her until their mouths were fused in passion.

And, right at that second, the security alarm went off.

CHAPTER FIVE

THE SHRIEK of the alarm shocked Mia into reality.

She struggled against Matthew's embrace. Instead of putting her down, his arms tightened around her and he moved quickly down the hall, into a room lined with bookcases.

A touch of his hand and one section slid away, revealing a small, lighted room.

He put her on her feet.

"There's a button on the wall beside the door. It works the lock from the inside. Hit that button, fast."

"But—"

"No but's, damn it! Do as you're told, and do it fast."

He pushed her inside the room, reached to the small of his back and pulled the gun from the waistband of his jeans.

"Lock the door."

"No. Matthew—"

He looked at her through the coldest eyes she'd ever seen. "All you are right now is a liability."

Without warning, tears rose in her eyes. Matthew's expression didn't change but he bent to her and gave her a quick, hard kiss on the mouth.

"Lock it," he said, stepping back.

She pushed the button. The door, as heavy as that of a bank vault, slid shut, cutting her off from the outside world and the shrill of the alarm.

Unnerving silence settled around her. Mia wrapped her arms around herself. Her teeth were chattering.

What was happening out there?

She put her ear to the door and felt the kiss of cold steel against her cheek. All she heard was the pounding beat of her blood in her ears.

She stepped back.

What kind of room was this? Door and walls of steel. No windows. An electronic keypad, lights blinking in a crazy-quilt of colors. A clock that showed the time around the world, a bank of built-in TV monitors. Cell phones, what looked like a fax machine, other electronic gadgets she couldn't identify.

Cabinets lined two walls. She opened them and saw tins of food, plastic jugs of water, first-aid supplies…

And weapons.

Handguns. Automatic rifles. Ammunition.

All this, in addition to the gun Matthew had pulled. The gun he'd had on him when he was making love to her.

She began to shake. Why was she surprised? She knew what he was, even if she'd somehow forgotten it for a little while.

He hadn't forgotten.

All you are is a liability.

Another tremor racked her body. She was cold. Terribly cold. How long would she be trapped in this place? What if something happened to Matthew? The button activated the lock, he'd said, but what if something went wrong? What if it didn't—

Something whirred in the wall. Mia whirled and pressed her ear to the door. Could your heart race this hard without bursting?

The whirring sound came again. With agonizing slowness, the door slid open. Matthew stood before her, hands on his hips, eyes unreadable.

No wounds. No injuries that she could see. It was wrong to feel such relief. Wrong to want to throw herself into his arms—but she was beginning to understand, all too well, the bizarre things stress could do to you in situations like this.

"You can come out now."

"What happened? Why did the alarm go off?"

The look on his face changed. It became…sheepish?

"It was an accident. Evalina—"

"Evalina?"

"Yeah. Evalina saw the Escalade going through the village, then turning down the road. She decided to drop by to see if it was really me, but she didn't punch in the security code in time."

Evalina, Mia thought, and hated herself for the swift rush of anger that swept through her.

"See, she knows I haven't been here in—in a very long time, so when she saw the SUV—"

"She was too thrilled to think straight." Mia started to flounce past him. "How nice for you bo—"

Matthew's hand closed around her shoulder. "What's the matter, baby?" His voice was lazy with amusement. "Jealous?"

"Saddened. That any woman would be so thrilled to see you that she'd break into your house."

A grin spread across his face. "You *are* jealous."

"You wish."

"Evalina," he said, "is my housekeeper."

His housekeeper. The explanation brought a flood of relief, and that only made her more angry. Why should she care?

"She comes by each week, cleans the place, whatever."

"It's none of my business what she does or what she is."

"You're right," he said, turning her to him. "It isn't. Just so we understand each other…" He paused. "If she were my lover, I wouldn't hide it. And I wouldn't have made a move on you."

Mia felt her face heat. "An unfortunate incident," she said stiffly.

"That I made the move?" A cool smile angled over his lips. "Or that you responded to it?"

He could tell by the burn in her cheeks that she knew better than to answer. Instead she pulled away from him. He let her do it. What had happened before was just what she'd called it, an unfortunate incident, and he sure as hell wouldn't let it happen again.

The best way to ensure that was to keep his hands off her.

"I assume you want to wash up." He jerked his head to the side. "The powder room's there. I'll wait for you."

"There's no need to wait for me."

"Of course there is." He gave her a taut smile. "A gentleman always escorts a lady to dinner."

"Is there a gentleman here? I hadn't noticed. Besides, I'm not hungry."

"You afraid of my cooking? Don't be. Evalina's making dinner."

"I said, I'm not hungry."

"Fine. You can sit and watch me eat."

"I won't do any such thing."

"Yes," he said grimly, "you will. You'll sit when I sit, walk when I walk, do what I do or I'll take the easy way out, tie you up, stash you here and inactivate the exit button. It's called a safe room," he said, reading the question in her eyes. "Come to think of it, maybe it's where I should keep you on general principle."

"On second thought," she said, her words dipped in acid, "I might be a bit hungry."

"Yeah," he said with a thin smile, "that's what I thought."

There was a formal dining room off the kitchen, but Matthew said they'd eat in the breakfast nook.

The king, Mia thought coldly, playing at being humble before his subjects… although Evalina seemed to treat him without any formality.

She was a round, cheerful woman who babbled incessantly as she prepared and served their meal.

Mia could only understand some of what she said. She'd taken two years of Spanish in college and a crash course before she went to work for Douglas in Colombia, but what people spoke in the sophisticated restaurants and offices of Cartagena had little in common with Evalina's Indian dialect.

Matthew, on the other hand, slipped into it easily. He grinned and laughed, and Evalina blushed with delight each time he did.

It was easy to see she had a crush on him.

If only she knew what he was really like, Mia thought as she ate. And she did eat, despite what she'd said. The food was wonderful, and she was famished. All she'd had since last night was coffee.

And now, night was closing in again.

She breathed a sigh of relief. Thank God for Evalina. Knowing the housekeeper was sleeping under the same roof would surely keep Matthew from—from—

What was the woman doing?

"Evalina?" Mia's fork clattered against her plate. "Evalina, wait…" Too late. A cheerful wave and the housekeeper slipped out the kitchen door. Mia stared at Matthew. "Where did she go?"

"Home."

He was mopping up the last of his *sancocho* with a chunk of *arepa,* as if the beef stew and corn meal biscuits were all he had on his mind.

"Doesn't she live here?"

"She lives in a village a couple of miles away."

"But I thought—"

"I know what you thought." He put down his fork, patted his lips with his napkin and flashed the kind of smile that turned her spine icy. "Sorry to disappoint you, baby, but you and I get to spend the night alone."

The man who'd joked with Evalina, complimented her on her cooking, was gone. He'd been replaced by the stranger who'd abducted her hours ago, a lifetime ago, from a dingy room in a nameless town.

Mia forced herself to look directly at him.

"If you try anything," she said, "I'll kill you."

A lazy grin curved his lips. "With what? Your bare hands?"

If she were a real agent, she could. Agents learned things like that. But she'd been trained in less than two weeks, snatched from her quiet secretarial desk in Intelligence and dropped into a nightmare.

Still, you didn't have to be a spy to know that backing away from a challenge was almost always a mistake.

"I'll do whatever I have to," she said, with what she thought was admirable coolness.

His smile disappeared as he shoved back his chair and got to his feet. "In that case," he said softly, "let's get started."

So much for bluffing.

His hand closed on her shoulder. She tried not to wince at the pressure.

"Stand up, Mia."

"No." The breath hissed from her lungs. "I swear, if you—"

"Stand up!"

The pain was almost unbearable. Gritting her teeth, she did as he'd ordered. He marched her from the kitchen, along the hall, back into the library. Her heart raced. Was he going to lock her in the safe room?

"Sit."

She sat, almost falling into a chair that faced an enormous fieldstone fireplace.

Matthew went to a cabinet. Took out a bottle and filled two balloon-shaped glasses. Held out one to her. She stared at it as if it might burst into flames at any minute.

"For God's sake," he growled, "it's brandy. Watch." He brought one glass to his lips, drank and swallowed, then did the same with the other and offered her the glass again. "Drink. Maybe it'll put some color back in your face."

She accepted the glass and took a small sip. The brandy was wonderful, warm and darkly rich. She shut her eyes, let its fire trickle down her throat, then licked the taste from her lips.

When she lifted her lashes, she saw Matthew watching her. Watching the progress of her tongue across her mouth.

His eyes met hers. "Good?" he said, his voice husky.

She nodded, and he sat down across from her, rolling his glass between his palms to heat the brandy before finally lifting it to his lips and taking a drink.

"It's time to get down to business."

Her heart thumped and she fought to keep the fear from showing in her face.

"We don't have any business."

"Wrong." His eyes narrowed. "We do."

The glass she'd wrapped both hands around began to tremble. The thing to do now was stay calm. Impress him with her honesty.

"Look," she said, striving for sincerity, "I understand that Douglas hired you to find me. Well, you found me. Tell him that. Call him up, tell him you did what he employed you to do and then tell him—tell him I don't want to go back to Cartagena." Did she sound sincere or desperate? "Then you just let me walk away."

He smiled thinly. "You walk away and I return to Cartagena, empty-handed."

"He'll still pay you. I mean, he'll see that you've done your job."

"He's not paying me."

Her eyes widened in surprise. "Then why…?"

"Why did you run away?"

She stood up. "We've been over this already. I left him."

"You ran. There's a difference. I want to know the reason."

"It's none of your business."

Matthew shot to his feet. A second later, he had her backed against the wall, his hands hard on her shoulders.

"Did he beat you?"

"No."

"Abuse you?"

"No. Damn it, let go of me."

"Is that the reason you became a thief?"

Mia's heart tripped. She thought of the miniature computer disk, concealed in the compact in her purse, and the information it contained.

"I don't know what you mean."

"Give me a break, baby. Hamilton told me everything. He caught you using the embassy mail pouch to smuggle cocaine. He put his neck on the line, covering for you, and you repay him by running away." His fingers bit into her flesh. "He doesn't know the reason, but I do. You ran with a stash of coke."

Did she laugh? Did she cry? Which was better, that Matthew think she'd stolen drugs...or that he learned that what she'd actually stolen would put Douglas Hamilton and a cartel drug lord in a federal prison forever?

It didn't matter.

She couldn't tell him anything. Besides, why would he give a damn? His job was to find her and bring her back to Cartagena.

No way was she going back. She knew, all too well, what awaited her there.

"Where is it? Where did you hide the dope?"

"Douglas lied," she said, looking straight into his eyes. "He told you that story so you'd find me and take me back, but it isn't true. There are no drugs. I ran from him because—because he wouldn't leave me alone."

Matthew's mouth twisted. "Those separate bedrooms," he said softly. "Hell, who could blame him? You're his fiancée."

She swallowed dryly. Maybe the truth, as much as she could reveal of it, would work.

"I worked for him in the States. When I came to Cartagena as his personal assistant, he said he had a big house with lots of empty rooms, and that it would be simpler if I lived there." *Simpler for her to get the dirt on him, too, as the Agency wanted, but she wasn't about to reveal any of that.*

Was it true? Matthew's eyes narrowed. It would explain the separate bedrooms, but he wasn't born yesterday.

"That's a nice story."

"It's what really happened. It was fine, for a while, but then—then he began saying things. Doing things." That was the truth, too. Just remembering it made her skin crawl—and now, it was time to start embellishing the story. "I told him I'd report him."

"And?"

"And, he said nobody would believe me. I'm a nobody. He's an army colonel with a brilliant career record."

Matthew let go of her and folded his arms. "So you decided to run."

"Yes."

"To take a little road trip through an area thick with bandits and insurgents." A muscle knotted in his jaw. "Exactly what most women do, when their fiancés suggest a little hanky-panky."

"Didn't you hear a word I just told you? He's not my fiancé."

He smiled coldly. He didn't believe her. Well, why would he? He was right. Taken at face value, her story was full of holes but what else could she tell him? She'd already come dangerously close to forgetting that he worked for a man who wanted what she had badly enough to kill her for it.

For all she knew, Matthew was toying with her. Good cop, bad cop. Nobody ever said that one actor couldn't take both roles…especially if he discovered that his prisoner trembled at his touch.

All at once, everything came into sharp focus. The darkness, closing in around the house. The silence. The seemingly endless forest and mountains that separated them from the rest of the world.

The man standing inches from her, arms folded so that every muscle in his torso stood in sharp relief.

Mia's heartbeat quickened. She took a step back.

"It's late. And I'm exhausted. Do you plan on letting me get some sleep, or is this interrogation going to go on until I collapse?"

"Interrogation?" His lips drew back from his teeth. "Baby, you don't know what the word means. All we're doing is having a conversation." He glanced at his watch. "But you're right. It's late and it's been one hell of a long day. I'd say yeah, it's definitely time to call it a night." He jerked his head toward the hallway. "Let's go to bed."

This time, her heart leaped into her throat.

"What—what does that mean?"

"Why, sugar, what do you think it means?"

His smile was one part sex, one part torment. He clasped her elbow but Mia refused to move.

"I'm not going to sleep with you, Mr. Knight."

"Can't get that name straight, can you, baby? It's Matthew. I mean, considering the circumstances, it would be foolish to stand on formalities."

"I said—"

"Yeah. I heard what you said." His tone, and his smile, hardened. So did the grip of his hand. "Seems to me we've been over this ground already. You'll do what you're told."

"No." Her voice was shaky but she forced her eyes to stay steady on his. "I won't sleep with—"

She gasped as his hand slipped to her wrist. His fingers dug into the tender flesh.

"Get moving."

"Matthew. Please—"

"Enough," he growled, picking her up and slinging her over his shoulder.

Shrieking, she pounded her fists against his back. He ignored her, carried her through the dark house and into an enormous room where he dumped her on her feet and flicked on the lights.

"My bedroom," he said tonelessly. "I hope the accommodations suit the lady."

"Don't do this! You aren't the kind of man who'd—who'd—"

"Aren't I?" Matthew locked the door. Then he turned to Mia, his eyes like slivers of emerald ice. "So far, you've accused me of being everything from muscle for hire to a killer. Why wouldn't I be happy to add rape to that list?"

"Because," she said, heart thumping. "Because—"

"Never mind." He strode past her, his body brushing hers, and fell back against the pillows ranged along the teak headboard of a massive bed. "I'm too tired for this crap. You want to make this out to be rape, that's your problem." He yawned, folded his arms behind his head and toed off his boots, which clattered to the tiled floor. "The shower's through there. You first."

"If you really think I'm going to—to get myself ready for—for—"

"Sweet mother of God," Matthew roared. Mia shrank back. Too late. He grabbed her, hustled her into a bathroom that seemed bigger than most people's houses, and turned on the overhead spray in a shower stall big enough for a party.

"Get your clothes off."

"I won't. I told you—"

"Then I'll do it."

She gasped and put up her fists, which would have made him laugh if he wasn't so damned tired.

Instead he swatted her hands away as if they were nothing but fruit flies, then undressed her with clinical efficiency, tugging off her T-shirt, peeling off her sandals, unbuttoning her jeans and pulling them down her legs.

She fought hard. Slapped. Kicked. Cried and shouted and called him names.

Well, he could hardly blame her but holy hell, he was exhausted and irritable. Most of all, he seemed to have forgotten how to think straight. He'd had it with trying to figure out if she was what Hamilton claimed or if she was something else.

Mostly he'd had it with trying to figure out how come he kept kissing this woman when so much pointed to her being bad news.

How come the feel of her skin under his hands was getting to him, even now?

The smell of her hair, too. That flower scent...

He had her down to her bra and panties. *Enough,* his weary brain said, and for once, he listened to it and let her go.

"Okay," he said grimly. "My turn."

He started to peel off his shirt. She gave a shocked sob and whirled toward the door.

"For heaven's sake," he snarled, and turned the lock. Then he picked her up and put her in the shower. She'd have to make it past him, if she made another break for freedom, and no way was he about to let that happen.

He tossed his shirt aside. Unzipped his jeans. Stepped out of them. Looked down at his Jockeys and decided to leave them on because as tired and angry as he was, he knew he was still on the edge of her having a predictable effect on him.

Then he stepped into the shower and closed the smoked glass door.

Mia shrank back. The look on her face almost made him laugh. The one time he'd stayed here, in a guest suite, the official who'd owned the house woke the place early in the morning with the kind of scream no grown man should make.

Everybody had come running.

They'd found the guy in this very shower stall, his back tight to the wall, a snake the size of the Amazon curled in the middle of the floor.

The way the guy had looked then was exactly the way Mia looked now.

Matthew reached past her. She all but bared her teeth. He plucked a bar of soap from the built-in shelf, made a point of showing it to her, then reached for a couple of washcloths.

She didn't move.

Okay. Let her play it her way.

He lathered one of the cloths, scrubbed the dust and sweat of the day and the road from his face, then from his body.

Mia watched, the way he figured an anthropologist would watch a tribal ritual.

He reached for the shampoo. Worked up a good lather. Rinsed off, but not the way he liked to, head back, eyes closed, because closing his eyes on the woman sharing this enclosed space would probably win him a knee in the groin.

Finished, he held out the soap and the other washcloth.

Mouth set, eyes narrowed, she took what he offered with no thanks. Rubbed the soap on the cloth. Began washing. Her face. Her throat. Her arms. And all the while, the water sluiced down on her skin, tiny drops beading on the swell of her breasts above her bra.

That plain white, demure, completely unseductive bra.

It was soaked. And translucent. Matthew could see her nipples.

His gaze dropped lower. Her panties were soaked with water, too. The dark shadow of the curls on her mons was clearly visible.

And, the scent of the soap…

How come it didn't smell like that on him?

He shifted his weight. *Get out of the shower, Matthew,* his head told him. *Right now, you idiot. Right now!*

Instead he watched her wash her hair. Watched the dark mass of it slither down her back as she raised her arms, put her head back, lifted her face to the spray.

Matthew groaned.

Mia's eyes flew open. She stared at him and then her gaze dropped lower, lower, dropped to his boxer shorts.

To the heavy bulge beneath them that he couldn't have controlled if his life depended on it.

She looked up. The shock of what he saw on her face jolted through him like a live wire.

The shampoo bottle fell from her hand.

"I'll get it," he said in a voice that bore no resemblance to his own.

He bent down, picked up the bottle, rose to his feet… Rose to his feet and put the bottle back on the shelf, and, hell, the only way to do that was to move closer to her.

"You missed a spot," he said thickly.

Her lips parted. "What?"

"You left some lather on your shoulder."

She didn't move. He stepped closer, skimmed her shoulder with his fingertips, then bent his head and put his mouth to her skin.

Her wet, sweet-smelling skin.

The sound that came from her throat was as soft as the whisper of the wind.

"You know why there was soap on your shoulder?" he said. She shook her head, her gaze fixed to his. "Because you can't take a proper shower with your clothes on."

He reached behind her. Found the clasp of her bra. She began to tremble as he opened it and drew the straps slowly down her arms.

His throat constricted. Her breasts were so beautiful. So beautiful.

Matthew bent his head. Kissed her arched throat. Kissed the lush curve of one breast, then drew the nipple into his mouth.

She moaned. Raised her hands. Put her palms flat against his chest.

He hooked his thumbs in the waistband of her panties. Gently worked them down her hips. Crouched before her so he could ease first one foot and then the other free.

He kissed her insteps. Her ankles. He raised his face, kissed her thighs and put his face against her. Against those feminine curls. And inhaled the scent of soap and woman and desire.

"Mia," he whispered, and he parted her labia with his tongue, touched it to the tiny, exotic bud that was hidden there, and she cried out, the sound high and wild and as exciting as her taste.

Her hands were in his hair. Her hips were undulating. She was weeping and he knew he was going to come any second and he didn't want that to happen, didn't want this to end before it had really begun.

He rose to his feet. Cupped her face and kissed her deeply, letting her taste the mingled flavors of his hunger and her desire.

Then he shut off the water, scooped her into his arms and headed for the bedroom.

CHAPTER SIX

A WASH of ivory moonlight lay over the huge bed.

Matthew carried Mia to it and lay her down in a sea of cool white linen. She opened her arms to him and he whispered her name as he went into her embrace.

He kissed her, kissed her again and again. Her honeyed taste filled his senses; he could kiss her forever, he thought, and never weary of doing it.

He caught her bottom lip between his teeth and bit gently into the soft flesh. She gasped and he soothed the hurt with kisses before slipping his tongue into her mouth.

She moaned at the sweet intrusion. That delicate sound, the arching of her body toward his, made him shut his eyes with pleasure.

Her breasts pressed lightly against the hard planes of his chest. Matthew cupped one, feathered his thumb over the nipple and exulted in her swift gasp of arousal.

"Do you like it when I touch your breasts?" he said hoarsely.

She answered by bringing his head to hers and kissing him, her mouth open and hot against his.

He was never going to make this last!

Sex was all about pleasure but it wasn't about losing

control, not until that final second of release. And yet, he was close to losing control now. He could feel it happening. Reality was slipping away. He could hear the pounding of his blood, thick in his veins.

His erection was so full it was almost painful.

Never, not in his entire life, had he wanted a woman as he wanted Mia.

Still cupping her breast, molding its shape with his hand, Matthew caught the nipple between his teeth, then sucked it into his mouth. Her cry rang into the still night.

"Matthew," she whispered. "Oh, Matthew…"

He rolled above her. Sent his hand skimming the length of her body. Her satin flesh was perfumed with desire.

Fragrant with it, because of him.

He had done this to her. Made her feel this way.

He was the one. Nobody else.

Her hands were on him. Her fingers moved over his shoulders and chest, stroked down his abdomen. Down and down again, and he caught his breath, anticipating her touch on his swollen flesh.

Her hand closed around him and Matthew threw back his head and groaned, every nerve-ending pulsing with the excitement of her caress.

It was almost more than he could take.

He had to stop her, he thought, and he closed his hand around hers…

And showed her, instead, how to move those smooth fingers along his steely length and drive him toward exquisite insanity.

His breath hissed through his teeth and he caught her hand again, brought it to his mouth, kissed it.

"Not yet," he said, "not yet, sweetheart."

He clasped her wrists, drew her arms high over her

head. Kissed the tender flesh he'd exposed. Bit it. Licked it, until he reached her wrists again. Until his mouth was once more at her breasts.

Until he slid his free hand between her legs.

Her cry almost made him come.

That sound, the glorious female surrender in it, the feel of her wet heat against his palm, damned near unmanned him.

Matthew closed his eyes and struggled for composure.

Mia was trembling beneath him. Sobbing his name. Moving, writhing against his hand.

"Mia," he said hoarsely, and he brushed his fingers over her clitoris.

She went wild, bucking against him, reaching up to kiss his mouth, to bite it, struggling to free her wrists from his grasp.

"No," she sobbed, "Matthew, no…"

"Yes," he said huskily, letting go of her wrists, sliding his hands beneath her. Raising her to him, opening her thighs wide so that she was entirely vulnerable.

She was so beautiful, here, in her very heart. The petals of her labia, the fragile bud within…

He kissed that bud. Tongued it. Worshipped her with his mouth. Felt the intensity of her response, her moans, her whispers, and when she gave a long, keening cry and lost herself in his arms, he felt something happen deep inside him, something that had less to do with sex and more to do with joy.

He moved up her body, held her close as she clung to him and wept. Then he clasped her face and kissed her mouth and when her eyes met his, when he saw her lips form his name, he entered her on a deep, sleek thrust.

Her hips lifted from the bed. Her legs rose and wrapped around his waist.

"Matthew," she said brokenly, and he began to move. Slowly. Deeply. Thrusting into her silken heat, then pulling back, and the pace of his lovemaking quickened, her cries grew more breathless and he felt it start, the incredible tension, the built-up of energy.

The long climb to the top, and then the moment when he stood poised on the very edge of the world...

Mia began to tremble. Her hands gripped his biceps, he saw her eyes blur with what was happening to her, what was happening to them both...

Then, only then, Matthew threw his head back and echoed her cry as he tumbled over the precipice.

They lay in a tangle of linen and moonlight, two strangers wrapped in each other's arms.

Cool air from the blades of a ceiling fan washed over them.

Maybe that was why Mia suddenly felt chilly... Or maybe it was something else. Maybe it was the sudden and dizzying return of sanity.

She opened her eyes. Stared up at the shadowed ceiling. Felt the powerful weight of Matthew's body on hers...and her blood ran cold.

Had she lost her mind?

She'd slept with two men in her entire life. A boy she'd dated in college and a man she'd almost become engaged to. She'd known each one for months before she let things get this far.

She'd known Matthew Knight for less than twenty-four hours.

And he wasn't a sweet-faced college kid or a doting

suitor. He was—he was hired muscle, come to take her back to Cartagena any way he could.

Hired by a man who wanted what she had in her compact. Wanted it enough to see her dead.

She must have done something, made a little sound, because Matthew lifted his head and looked at her.

"What's the matter?"

"Nothing," she said quickly. "Nothing's the matter."

"I'm too heavy for you," he said, and rolled off her. She began to move away but he drew her into his arms.

"Hey," he said softly.

She forced a smile. "Hey, yourself."

He gave her a soft kiss. *How could a man like him be so tender?* "You sure you're okay?"

No, she thought, I'm not. But she knew what he was asking.

"Yes. I'm fine."

"Because—" He gave a husky laugh. "Because if that was a little too fast—"

It wasn't. It had been wonderful. Incredible. Incredible sex, with a man who'd abducted her…

"No," she said, "no, it was fine."

"Ah," he said solemnly, "I get it. You're fine, and the sex was fine. So, let's see, on a scale of one to ten, what's that register? A four?"

"No. Honestly. I only meant—"

"You meant," he said quietly, "you don't know what the hell you're doing, lying here in my arms."

She felt the color rush into her face. Foolish, because what was there to blush about, considering what they'd just done?

"I don't…" She cleared her throat. "I don't really want to talk about it, Matthew."

She tried to move, but his arms tightened around her.

"Good." His tone roughened. "Neither do I, because I don't have any answers, either." He rolled her onto her back, clasping her wrists so her hands were at her sides, his eyes a luminous emerald green in the moonlight. "All I know is that I wanted to make love to you as soon as I saw you."

"Was that before or after you broke into my room?"

He let go of her hand, caught hold of her face, held it so she had no choice but to meet his gaze.

"Yeah," he said gruffly, "I broke in. I forced you to go with me." She started to twist away but he wouldn't let her. His fingers dug into her jaw. "And you still have something you got in Cartagena. I don't know what it is. I don't even know who you are." A muscle knotted in his jaw; his eyes moved over her face, lingering on her parted lips, then rose to meet her gaze again. "But I've never wanted a woman the way I want you."

"That's a charming line. Does it always wor—"

She gasped as he kissed her, his mouth ruthless against hers. She struggled but he showed her no mercy until, to her horror, she felt herself giving in to his kiss, felt her lips moving against his, her heartbeat quickening as it had before.

"You see?" he whispered, stroking his hand down her body. "It's the same for you."

"It's not. It's not! I don't want you. I don't—"

He kissed her, his mouth brushing lightly over hers.

"One way or another," he said, "I've been a soldier all my life. I live by a code, Mia. Call it a code of honor, call it discipline—any name you give it, it means the same thing. I honor my commitments."

"Meaning," she said, a little catch in her voice, "don't expect special treatment, just because we've—we've—"

"Meaning," he said harshly, "this is the first time I've broken that code. I shouldn't have made love to you." His voice softened; he stroked her hair back from her face and this time, when he kissed her, the kiss was so tender she felt her heart melt. "The truth is, I don't know what happens next. I only know that talking never accomplishes anything."

His hand moved and covered her breast. His thumb brushed her nipple, and the liquid tug it elicited deep in her belly was intense enough to make her moan.

"But this," he said in a low, hot voice, "this will."

He kissed her again and again, until she knew he was right. Nothing mattered but him and the way she felt when he touched her. The way he groaned under the stroke of her hand. The way he tasted, all salt and passion and clean, powerful man, when she kissed him.

When at last, Matthew slid into her, deep into her, he rode her until she was blind to everything but him.

Sweat glistened on his shoulders. Mia kissed his salty skin, clasped his hips, levered herself up to meet his powerful thrusts.

The crest of the wave grew higher and higher. She was frantic to ride it to shore but Matthew wouldn't let her. She begged for him to end it and, at last, he did, crying out with her as she came apart and shattered in his arms.

She collapsed against him, weeping with joy, with despair, with so many emotions they threatened to destroy her.

Matthew held her close, his heart racing against hers.

"Mia," he said softly, but she shook her head.

She wasn't going to think about anything. Not now.

Instead she kissed his mouth, then fell asleep safe in his arms.

She awoke as the moon was setting.

Only the faintest light seeped into the room. Beyond the massive bed, the balcony door stood open to the soft whispers of the forest and the night.

Matthew had rolled onto his belly. He lay with one arm wound around her waist; his thigh was draped across hers. His breath was soft on her throat and his silky hair tickled her cheek.

Mia closed her eyes.

She thought of what had happened in his bed. Of how she'd given herself to him, again and again.

Oh God, she thought. *God, what's happened to me?*

The wildness of her passion stunned her. She'd never been like this. Never.

She thought of the two lovers in her past. Two very nice, very normal men, one studying to be a teacher, the other a lawyer with an office and a nine-to-five existence.

She'd known all there was to know about them both. Where they lived. What books they read, what music they listened to. She knew so much about them that when she'd finally slept with them, nothing, not even the sex, had seemed new.

What she'd done with Matthew, the sex…

Her breath hitched. The truth was, she'd never even had an orgasm until tonight.

Everything she'd done with Matthew was new and exciting and dangerous, just as he was dangerous.

He was a beautiful animal, wild and incapable of being tamed.

She couldn't picture him in captivity, trapped behind a desk in the nine-to-five world.

He'd spent most of his life as a soldier, he'd said, but she couldn't even see him in that role, wearing a pressed uniform, marching in lock-step, taking orders and saluting.

This was who Matthew Knight was.

A man who'd abduct a woman. Strip search her. Force her to do his bidding. Except—except, he hadn't forced her to come apart at his touch. He hadn't forced her to do anything in bed.

She'd been a willing participant, exchanging caress for caress and kiss for kiss. It made her blush to think of the things she'd done, the way she'd pleaded for him to drive deep into her as he took her on a journey she'd never made before.

A knot of fear lodged in her belly.

She'd slept with a stranger. Done things she wished she could forget. And the only thing she really knew about him was that he'd been sent to bring her back to certain death at the hands of his employer...

Or do the job himself.

The chill in her belly turned to ice.

She checked Matthew again. He was still sleeping. He looked peaceful—and beautiful. His face, his body. He was a dark angel and yet, his touch could be tender, his mouth sweet.

One final caress, she thought, her heart pounding with the urgency of it, one last whisper of her lips against his...

No! She had her sanity back. Was she going to toss it away again?

Holding her breath, Mia moved out from under his arm. Straightened her leg until it slid from beneath his.

She sat up, pushed back the light duvet Matthew had drawn up over them.

Carefully, quietly, she slipped from the bed.

Where were her clothes? In the bathroom. Heat rushed to her face as she remembered Matthew undressing her.

How he'd forced her to stand naked in front of him.

How terrible it had been…

Oh God, how exciting it had been! The way he'd stripped her. Gotten her wet. Removed her bra and panties and then made love to her. She'd never believed sex could be so powerful.

Was that why she was running? To save her life…or to save her soul? To get away from a man who might hurt her, or to escape what he'd taught her about herself? About sensuality, and what it was like to be stroked until you purred.

A year ago, she'd led such a normal life. Get up, get dressed, go to her job as secretary in a dreary government office that dealt in Intelligence but was really all about mind-boggling statistics.

But "normal" and "dreary" were fine with her. Her childhood had been neither. Her father had been a gambler, her mother was always sickly…

She closed her eyes.

The truth was, her mother was an alcoholic. Growing up, she'd never known what the next day would bring. She'd longed for a quiet, predictable life and she'd found one.

And then, one morning, her boss said she was wanted on the sixteenth floor. Take the freight elevator, he'd said. Mia thought that was strange but she did as he'd instructed, and stepped into a world she hadn't known existed.

It was a world called the Agency.

A woman in a black silk suit greeted her, led her down the hall to an enormous office and introduced her to a man she addressed as the Director.

The Director made small talk for a few minutes. Then his expression turned grave.

Ms. Palmieri, he'd said, *you worked for Colonel Douglas Hamilton for the year he was stationed here, in Washington.*

Yes, she'd said, *that's right, I did.*

According to our records, Colonel Hamilton was very pleased with you.

With my work? she'd said, because the truth was, Hamilton hadn't been happy with other things, like the way she'd avoided working late at night because something in the way he looked at her made her uncomfortable. *Yes,* she'd replied, *I believe he was.*

The Director had leaned forward.

Ms. Palmieri, he'd said, *I'm going to offer you an opportunity to serve your country.*

Mia shuddered.

But her country hadn't served her. She'd discovered she was expendable. The man she'd slept with was the final proof. And she'd slept with him. Made love with him…

Sex. Not love. Sex. She didn't know why the distinction was important, but it was.

Her small overnight bag was on the chair but she wasn't going to risk waking Matthew by rustling through it. For all she knew, he was a light sleeper.

His closet took up an entire wall. She held her breath as she slid the doors open, but he didn't stir. Clothing was neatly folded on shelves. She pulled on a T-shirt and sweatpants, then rolled them to her knees.

She'd have to do without shoes.

Barely breathing, clutching the suitcase and her purse, she tiptoed from the room. Down the endless hall. Into the foyer. The front door was just ahead. Was the alarm really rigged to sound even if you were leaving the house? She had to hope not. Otherwise, she'd have to pray she reached the SUV before Matthew came running.

He'd left his keys on a small table near the door. The floor was cool under her feet as she went to it and ran her hand over the surface.

No keys. But that was impossible. She felt along the top of the table again. Still nothing. How could that be? She was sure she'd seen him drop the—

The hundreds of crystal prisms in the foyer's grand chandelier blazed to life. Mia cried out, threw up her hand to shade her eyes from its bright glare…

And saw Matthew, half a dozen feet away, wearing only a pair of unzipped jeans, leaning back against the wall with a look on his face that reminded her of how dangerous he actually was.

"Is this what you're looking for, baby?" he said coldly.

The keys dangled from the fingers of his raised hand.

CHAPTER SEVEN

HE'D TAKEN her by surprise.

Good. That was exactly what he wanted.

Long moments ago, when he'd awakened to find Mia stirring beside him, his reaction had been instantaneous.

Male, and instantaneous. Even after making love to her twice, he awoke hard and eager to take her again.

He knew that didn't make sense. She was his prisoner. She was a thief. She dealt in drugs.

All another man had done was ask him to find her.

But he wanted her. Making love with her hadn't ended his hunger, it had only increased it.

There were so many things they hadn't done. Things he wanted to do while he watched her face. He wanted to go more slowly, kiss his way down her body, seek out all the shadowed parts of her and explore them.

Crazy as it seemed, making love with Mia had been different. She'd been innocent and abandoned, tender and wild, and in those last minutes of his possession, when she began to tremble beneath him, he'd felt as if he were standing on the edge of the universe.

No. None of it made sense, but he was a man of

action, not introspect. Why try to figure out what would cause such powerful sexual attraction?

Living it was all that mattered.

He'd been on the verge of doing just that a few minutes ago, of drawing her closer and kissing her, but something had stopped him.

Her caution, maybe.

She'd held herself as if she were made of glass.

He'd told himself he was overreacting. She thought he was asleep. She didn't want to wake him. Maybe she had to go to the bathroom, and she was working up to easing from the bed without disturbing him.

Wrong.

When she finally slipped out from under his arm, she didn't head for the bathroom, she headed for his closet.

He watched through slitted eyes as she chose a T-shirt and sweatpants and put them on.

That was when he understood, Mia was getting ready to run away. To leave him.

He told himself that was a crazy way to label it. He'd taken her captive, brought her here against her will. As she saw it, this was their own war, and a POW's first obligation was to try to escape.

All nicely logical, except she wasn't his prisoner of war anymore. She was—she was—

Damn it, what was she? A woman he'd taken to bed, that was all. What they'd done was have sex. Nothing more, nothing less—and he'd been a fool to have fallen asleep with her in his arms as if they were lovers instead of tying her up, the way he'd planned.

She'd let him seduce her. Or maybe it was the other way around. Maybe it had all been deliberate. She'd wanted him off his guard and he, fool that he was, had obliged.

And yet—and yet, even when he'd followed her down the hall, some foolish part of him had been hoping she'd just gone for a glass of water. A cup of tea.

Sure, he thought grimly, seeing the look of horror on her face as she saw him, of course. A woman would definitely go for a glass of water with her overnight case in her hand.

"Matthew." She gave a little laugh. "You're awake."

He didn't answer. He saw her throat constrict as she swallowed.

"I was just—I was just—"

"I know what you were 'just,'" he said coldly, waggling the keys. "You were just looking for these."

Her eyes flicked away from his. "No. I wasn't. Why would I—"

She gasped and fell back as he came toward her; she hit the wall and he caught her by the shoulders.

"I don't know, baby. You tell me."

"I—I was looking for—for my purse. I thought I'd left it on—on the table, and—"

"That purse?" he said silkily. "The one hanging from your shoulder?"

She stared at him. "Look. I know how this seems, but—"

"How does it seem, Mia? You tell me."

"There's a simple explanation. If you give me a minute, I—" She cried out as he lifted her to her toes. "Matthew. You're hurting me."

"Isn't it usually the guy who's accused of 'slam, bam, thank you, ma'am'?"

Her cheeks colored. "That's vulgar."

"And we wouldn't want to be vulgar, would we?" His mouth thinned. "I mean, that sure as hell wouldn't suit the kind of woman who screws a man in hopes it'll make him careless."

"You're disgusting!"

"I'm just telling it like it is. We went to bed together, you screwed my brains out—"

Her hand flew through the air and struck his cheek with enough force to make his head snap back. Matthew grabbed her wrist, dragged her arm behind her back and pulled her tightly against him.

"You like to play rough? Hell, baby, I'm into that if you are."

"Let go of me!"

"Sure. Once I've got you someplace nice and safe."

He started back down the hall, half dragging her along beside him, propelled her into the bedroom and hit a wall switch that turned on the lights. Then he grabbed her suitcase and purse and shoved her toward the bed.

He could see the terror in her eyes. Good, he thought viciously. She damned well should be terrified.

"Get on the bed."

"Please. Matthew—"

"On the bed," he barked. She scrambled into the middle of the mattress, as if putting a few inches of distance between them would keep her safe. "One move," he said, pointing his finger at her, "just one, and you'll regret it."

"If you'd just listen—"

"You give me two seconds of trouble, I'll lock you in the safe room." His smile was thin and cold. "After I empty it of weapons, of course, then lock it, permanently, from the outside. And then, who knows, baby? I might just forget I put you there."

Mia ran to the balcony door as he strode from the

room. It was locked. She didn't see a key or a bolt but the door was locked.

"Open," she said, pulling at the knob with both hands. "Damn you, open—"

She shrieked as Matthew's arms closed around her. He carried her back to the bed, dumped her on it and tossed a pair of handcuffs on the nightstand.

A sob burst from her throat. "No. Matthew—"

"Lie down and hold your hands above your head."

"Matthew. I implore you. Whatever Douglas told you—"

His head came up. She had never seen eyes as empty as his.

"Yeah," he said softly, "that's the problem, isn't it? I forgot what old Dougie told me about you and your little games."

"It isn't true. I never—"

"Never played all your bedroom tricks on him? Do us both a favor, baby. Don't bother lying. I know all about it." His jaw tightened. "It's too bad I didn't remember sooner, but you're good, I have to give you that." He picked up the cuffs. The harsh light glinted off their bright silver surface. "Hands," he barked.

She didn't move. Matthew cursed, grabbed her left wrist, braceleted it with steel, brought it behind the bedpost and did the same to her right. The ratcheting sound of the cuffs closing was like a prison door slamming shut.

"Matthew." Tears were streaming down Mia's face. "Matthew, I swear—"

Grimly he pulled her hands over her head, looped the rope through the cuffs and secured it to the bedpost. He gave the rope a tug and nodded his approval.

"That'll do it."

The sensation of being tied, of having her arms fixed above her head, was terrifying. Mia began to weep as he went to the bedroom door and shut it.

"Matthew," she sobbed as he strode toward her, "please, please, please!"

He stripped off his jeans. He was aroused and erect, and he didn't give a damn if she saw it.

Hell, he wanted her to see it.

Let her fear him. Let her.

She shrank away as he climbed onto the bed beside her.

"Don't," she whispered.

"Don't what?" he said coldly. "Don't do this?"

Eyes locked to hers, he reached out, cupped her breast, let his hand drift down her torso, then slipped it between her thighs.

She moaned. Not as she'd moaned for him earlier. Not with desire. She moaned with fear.

That was fine with him.

"Keep quiet," he said, hitting the light switch near the bed and plunging the room into darkness. "Or I'll tape your mouth shut."

Mia stared into the blackness. She could just make out his hulking shape. He would tape her mouth shut. He would.

She rolled her lips together. Pressed down hard on them to stifle the sobs mounting in her throat.

His shadowed shape moved. Flattened, and the mattress shifted.

He was lying down next to her.

A heartbeat later, she heard the soft chuff of his breath. Her jailer was asleep.

* * *

Matthew slept exactly as he'd intended. Twenty minutes. Not a second more, not a second less. He woke as refreshed as if he'd slept the entire night.

It was something he'd learned to do when he was in Special Forces. Cam had been the first one to go in for eastern stuff. Breathing exercises. Tai chi of the mind, he called it, and Matthew and Alex had both laughed...

Until they saw that it worked.

Matthew had explored further and discovered a handful of ancient Zen techniques. One taught you to separate your mind from your body. It had helped him save his sanity in this very country when he and Alita had been tortured.

The other was a mind-exercise that induced sleep. Deep sleep, the kind you needed when all you had were minutes instead of hours.

It had worked. He was well-rested. He had to be because by the time dawn roused the sleeping forest, he needed to be ready with a plan.

What would be the most effective way to force the truth from his prisoner? And that was what she was. How could he have deluded himself into seeing her as something else?

She wasn't a beautiful woman he'd met at a party. She was a criminal, or she damned well would have been if her lover hadn't protected her. That he'd forgotten that proved how far removed he was from his days as a spook.

Okay. He'd made a mistake, but he wouldn't make any others.

He lay still in the dark, feeling the strength flowing through his body, the cobwebs clearing from his mind. He was fine now.

She was the subject, this was an assignment and—

And, what was that sound?

Mia was weeping.

Quietly. So quietly that it was hardly more than a thickness in the inhalation of her breath but yes, she was weeping.

Let her, he thought coldly.

She'd used him, and he didn't like it. Or maybe it was that he didn't like himself, for being dumb enough to let it happen.

Either way, let her cry.

Let her lie beside him, arms jerked into a position that wouldn't leave lasting damage but was surely uncomfortable. Let her imagination work overtime, painting vivid pictures of what he was going to do to her…

Of what he'd already done.

Held her in his arms. Kissed her mouth, tasted her sweetness on his tongue. Put his lips to her breasts, sucked on her nipples as he stroked her. As he put his hand between her thighs, caught the warm dew of her femininity in his palm. As he lifted her legs over his shoulders, entered her, slowly, slowly, exulted in her moans, her cries, the way her muscles had tightened around him, the way she'd sobbed his name as she came…

Goddammit!

He sat up and swung toward her.

"Stop that crying," he said gruffly.

Her breath hitched. He could tell she was trying to obey his command but she couldn't. Well, so what? A woman's crying had never killed anybody.

Except, maybe, the man listening.

"Did you hear what I said? Stop sniveling. It pisses me off and, trust me, you don't want to piss me off any more than you already have."

She made a sound he knew meant she was trying to choke back her tears. It didn't help. If anything, her weeping intensified.

Matthew shot to his feet, marched across the floor and slammed the bathroom door behind him.

He stood at the sink for a long time, hands clutching the rim, head bowed. Then he flicked on the light and stared into the mirror. He looked like a man who'd just had a quick glimpse of hell.

He turned on the shower. Stepped under the spray, turned it as hot as he could bear it, then turned it icy-cold. He bowed his head, let the water beat down on his neck and shoulders. Turned on the side-sprays and let them do their work on the muscles in his back and his hips.

It seemed like a hundred years ago, he'd stood in this same shower stall, Mia before him, watching the water turn her hair to silk, watching it turn her bra translucent…

Matthew mouthed a harsh obscenity.

To hell with that.

He needed a plan. He had to shake the truth loose from her. Either she had dope on her or she didn't. Then he'd decide whether to take her back to Hamilton or send her to the States or—or—

Crap!

He shut off the sprays, stepped from the stall, dried off. Took a deep breath. Then he wrapped the towel around his waist and flung open the bathroom door.

Light spilled into the bedroom.

He saw Mia, lying as he'd left her, arms raised above her head, wrists manacled. Her head drooped but the second the light hit her, her chin came up. Her face was tear-streaked but the old defiance was back, manifested in the jut of her chin and the glitter in her swollen eyes.

Something shapeless and dark stretched feathery wings deep inside him.

He strode toward her, opened the cuffs that secured her to the bedpost and drew her arms down.

She whimpered in distress and he told himself that the stab of pain he felt on hearing it was meaningless, just a whisper of human empathy, that was all.

He wouldn't have been troubled by it back in his Agency days, but wasn't that one of the reasons he'd left? Because the Agency was a black hole that had damned near sucked the humanity out of him?

No way did his reaction have anything to do with Mia. He'd have felt like this for anyone.

Yeah. Sure you would.

Matthew cleared his throat. "You have a lactic acid build-up in your muscles," he said crisply. "It'll ease in a couple of minutes."

She didn't answer. He clasped her shoulders. She was trembling, and tried to jerk away.

"Don't be an idiot," he growled. "Let me get some circulation back. You'll feel better."

He ran his hands up and down her arms, gently kneading her flesh. Her trembling stopped but there were still tears in her eyes.

How come seeing them put a knot in his throat?

A muscle jumped in his cheek. He touched the chafe marks the cuffs had left on her wrists.

"You shouldn't have struggled against the cuffs."

She didn't answer. Fine. He'd made his point, scared her into compliancy just as he'd intended.

The truth was, he wouldn't need the cuffs anymore

tonight. She was going to be docile. Besides, he was wide awake. He could keep an eye on her. No sweat.

"Better?"

Still no answer. He took her hands in his. They felt icy. It wasn't cold in the bedroom. The overhead fan was doing its thing, moving the night air in easy circles, cooling the room without chilling it.

He put his hand against her cheek. It was cold, too. Shock? Out and out physical shock? No. She had none of the other signs.

Emotional shock, then. That made sense. It explained her trembling, her acquiescence...

And those tears, welling in her eyes.

"Hell," he muttered.

He put his arms around her. She came to life in a second, shoving against his chest and shoulders.

So much for being docile, he thought, and almost laughed at how good it made him feel to see the fight in her return.

"Easy," he said, wrapping her tightly in his arms, but she kept struggling and they tumbled sideways on the bed. "I'm not going to hurt you."

She got one hand free and swung at him. There was no force behind the blow—she couldn't get her arm back far enough for that—but her knuckles grazed his chin.

"Damn it," he growled, "I said I wasn't going to hurt you!"

He caught her hand, tucked it between them and held her in place with one arm while he tugged up the sheet and the duvet.

She was still shaking.

Nerves, rage, fear... Whatever it was, he had to stop it.

Matthew drew her flush against his body. She fought

hard, wriggling in his embrace, but he held her tight, stroked his hand down her back, then brushed her tangled curls from her forehead.

Little by little, she stopped fighting him.

He felt the chill seep from her body.

Felt her tremors slow.

And felt, sweet Jesus, felt the wonder of having her in his arms again.

He shut his eyes. Dipped his nose into her hair and inhaled its scent. The aroma shot through his blood. A magnum of Dom Perignon couldn't have had a more powerful effect.

Her heart was beating hard against his.

Once, years ago, when he was eight or nine, still innocent of the world's evils, he'd been riding the ranch with Cam and Alex. They were playing a game they loved, pretending to be Comanche warriors, proud descendents of the mother they hardly remembered.

Matthew's horse had snorted and reared.

Even then, he was a good rider. He'd steadied the animal, checked around—rattlesnakes were always a threat and horses were terrified of them—and saw, in the grass just ahead, not a snake but a nest.

It was a small, commonplace thing made of twigs and dead grass, but it held a miracle. A tiny, defenseless, unfledged bird.

He'd dismounted, taken the baby carefully in his hand and felt its tiny heart racing with terror.

None of them knew what to do. Finally he'd put the nest into a tree, dug up a couple of worms and put them in beside the bird.

When he went back, two days later, the tiny creature lay motionless, its heart forever stilled.

Now, all these years later, Mia's heart raced with fear, just like that baby bird's.

Maybe she was all the things Hamilton had said. Or maybe there were reasons to explain whatever she'd done. Maybe all he had to do was ask her…

Matthew swallowed hard.

Maybe it didn't matter.

He wasn't a saint. He'd done things he wouldn't even admit to himself.

"Mia," he said huskily, "baby, I'm sorry I frightened you."

She looked up at him, eyes wet and glittering with tears.

"Douglas lied to you," she said in a thready whisper.

"Never mind. I don't have the right to sit in judgment on you."

"You'd have every right, if I'd tried to smuggle cocaine." Her voice broke. "I didn't. I never smuggled drugs. Never!"

"Hush."

Matthew cupped her face and kissed the tears from her eyes. He brushed his lips over hers. Then he drew her close and rocked her in his arms.

He could feel the last of her tension slipping away.

Another kiss, then. Another whisper of his mouth on hers. It didn't mean anything. He only wanted to hold her and soothe her.

She was so warm. So soft.

One more kiss. Just one, and if, by chance, her mouth clung to his, if she sighed and slid her arms around his neck…

"Mia," he whispered, "baby."

Her hands crept up his chest. Over his shoulders.

Her fingers linked at his nape. When he kissed her, her mouth opened to his.

Before he could think, his hand was under her shirt, seeking her breast, cupping it. She moaned and his kiss deepened.

Suddenly, she drew back. Her eyes, filled with doubt, met his.

"I don't know who you are, Matthew. I don't know what you are. This is—it's crazy. We can't. We shouldn't—"

She broke off in midsentence. On a desperate sob, she clasped his face between her hands, brought his mouth to hers and kissed him with a passion that set him on fire.

Together, they pulled off her clothes. She rose to him as he knelt between her thighs and buried himself inside her on one long, silken thrust.

She was weeping at the end. Weeping with happiness.

And Matthew was filled with joy.

CHAPTER EIGHT

A WHILE AGO, Matthew had used an ancient meditation technique to find restful slumber.

Now, all he needed was to make love with Mia, then have her fall asleep in his arms.

There were still so many unanswered questions…but right now, all that mattered was this. Mia, warm and soft in his embrace.

He felt her body relax against his. He kissed her and she sighed and rolled to her side, her head still on his shoulder. Matthew drew her closely against him.

All those questions, he thought…

And fell with her, into sleep.

In the pale silver light just before dawn, as soft birdcalls sounded in the forest, Mia woke in Matthew's arms, pressed back against him.

His mouth was on her nape.

His hands cupped her breasts.

And the hot, silken-steel fullness of his erection nudged at the juncture of her thighs.

She started to turn in his arms, but he wouldn't let

her. Instead he pushed into her, his penetration deep and powerful.

No preliminaries.

There was no need for any. She was ready and eager for his possession.

She cried out; her head fell back against his shoulder as he began to move, faster and faster, and when he groaned and sank his teeth into her flesh, she flew with him into the golden sun.

Long moments later, he turned her in his arms. Her eyes were coals, burning into his.

"Matthew," she whispered.

She put her hand against his cheek. He caught it, brought the palm to his lips and kissed it.

And lay watching her, holding her, long after she drifted back to sleep.

He must have slept, too, because the next thing he knew, the sun was approaching its zenith.

Mia was still in his arms.

A strand of dark hair was caught against the corner of her mouth and he eased it away with his fingertip, then kissed the spot where it had been.

It felt so good, holding her like this. Being with her in this house he'd once expected to love and had, instead, hated.

Foolish. A house was only a house, he understood that now. If a man was going to have bad dreams, it didn't matter where he was. The dreams would keep coming until he chased them out of his head.

Mia being here with him had made him feel different about the house, even about Colombia.

The problem was, he still felt the same about himself.

Alita. The name came to him as it so often did. He hadn't been able to save her.

Would he be able to save Mia?

She was running from something, but he couldn't protect her until he knew what that something was. She wasn't a thief. She didn't deal in drugs. He'd have staked his life on both things.

Then, why was she on the run? Why would she be in danger from the cartel? If there was nothing between her and Hamilton, why did he want her back?

Why had he lied, and clearly said that there was?

Matthew let out a long breath.

Pieces of the puzzle were missing. The only certainty was that he'd do whatever it took to shield the woman lying in his arms. She needed his protection. Needed him.

And he—he—

No. Hell, no. He didn't need her. He wanted her, yes. Wanted her more than he'd ever wanted a woman, but need her? Uh uh. He'd never needed anybody.

He never would.

Matthew frowned. Carefully, he eased his arm from under her shoulders. Took one last look at her face, and then he rose, pulled on a pair of faded denim shorts, and left the room.

Mia was dreaming.

She was walking down a dark, narrow corridor with Matthew.

Where are we going? she said, but he was mute.

A man stood at the end of the corridor. She couldn't see his face but she knew who it was.

Please, she said to Matthew, *don't make me go to him.*

Matthew kept walking, his hand tightening on hers…

Heart pounding, Mia shot up in bed. Sunlight streamed in the window, dappling the pink petals of the perfect wild orchid lying on the pillow next to hers.

The last vestiges of the bad dream slipped away. Smiling, she took the orchid and brought it to her lips.

Last night was the only reality that mattered. Her smile tilted. Unless it, too, was only a dream…

But it wasn't. She knew that as soon as she showered and dressed, followed the rich aroma of fresh coffee to the kitchen, and saw Matthew.

He stood with his back to her in the open deck door, his hands tucked into the back pockets of his denim shorts, his shoulders stretching the confines of his cotton T-shirt.

Mia's heart turned over. This beautiful man, this strong and incredible man, was her lover.

Matthew turned and looked at her. His eyes were unreadable, his jaw was tight. For an instant, the uncertainty came back. She'd slept with him, explored his body as he'd explored hers, and she still didn't know anything about him, or why Douglas had chosen him to hunt her down…

"Good morning," he said softly, and everything changed, his eyes, his expression, and when he opened his arms, she stopped thinking and flew into his embrace.

"I'm sorry I slept so late," she said, smiling up at him.

"Mmm." His arms tightened around her. "You should be. Thanks to you, I'm starving."

"You should have had breakfast without me."

His smile was slow and sexy. "I'm not talking about breakfast," he said softly, and gave her an unhurried, coffee-flavored kiss.

He led her onto the deck. She'd only glimpsed it yesterday. Now, she saw that it ran the length of the house. Low stone walls bordered its perimeter. The air was redolent with the scent of flowers that overflowed terra cotta planters scattered everywhere.

"This is wonderful," Mia said softly.

Matthew brought her hand to his lips. "I thought we'd have breakfast out here."

"Yes. That would be perfect."

They ate at a glass table, shielded from the sun by a huge blue umbrella. Evalina had gone to the local native market but she'd left their meal ready for them: covered dishes of scrambled eggs, bacon and tortillas.

"What is this place?" Mia asked. "Where are we?"

"We're in the Andes. A mountain range called the Corillera Oriental."

"It's like being on top of the world."

He smiled. "The locals call it Cachalú. Land of the Sky."

"And all of it's yours?"

His smile became a grin. "Not quite all, but a big piece of it, yeah."

"But you're North American."

His smile faded. "I spent some time here, long ago."

"Here? At this house, you mean?"

He shook his head. "I was in the country, and I spent a couple of days here, on business. Someone else owned it then."

"A friend?"

"Just someone I knew. Not really what I'd call a friend." He paused. "A guy I, ah, I met through work."

"I thought you said you were a soldier."

"I was." The last remnant of his smile disappeared. "It's ancient history."

Chastened, Mia sat back. "Matthew, I'm sorry. I didn't mean to pry."

He reached for her hand and wound her fingers through his. "No, baby, I'm the one who's sorry. It's just that the time I spent here wasn't... I'm not much for reliving the past, you know?" He smiled again, though she could tell that it was forced. "Besides, why should we talk about me when we can talk about you?"

They couldn't talk about her. He'd ask questions and she couldn't give him answers. Not without being absolutely certain of the real reason he'd been looking for her.

And if her heart was right, if Matthew didn't know the truth about Douglas, telling him too much would put him in danger, too.

"There's not much to talk about," she said with a quick smile.

Matthew brought her hand to his mouth. "I'll bet there is. What's your favorite ice cream flavor? Who's gonna win the pennant this year? Do you like to watch football? Can you understand a word Bob Dylan says? How do you feel about Mahler?"

"Mahler?" she said, lifting her eyebrows.

"Yeah. Too much—or not enough?"

Mia laughed. "Chocolate," she said, "the Red Sox. Yes, no, too much."

Matthew grinned. "A woman who knows her own mind. I like that."

"What about you?"

"Strawberry. The Yankees. Yes, no—"

"I meant, why did Douglas hire you to come after me?"

She hadn't meant to say it, the words just tumbled out. She blinked and saw Matthew's smile disappear.

"Matthew. I didn't mean—"

"That's okay. Straight to the nitty-gritty. Hell, why not?" The muscle in his jaw knotted. "For instance, what made you come to Colombia?"

She stared at him. The truth leaped to the tip of her tongue. She longed to tell it to him. To explain that one day she'd been a secretary and the next, a nameless agency had turned her into a spy.

"It's a simple question, baby. How about answering it?"

Matthew was still smiling, but his eyes had narrowed in that way she'd come to know meant he was analyzing every word. Okay. She'd tell him the truth—as much as she could.

"It was—I guess you'd call it a fluke. I was a secretary in Washington. And then my boss told me there was an opening in Cartagena. He asked if I'd be interested."

"And you said sure, just like that."

"Yes. Just like—"

"Had you applied for a transfer?"

"Well, no."

"Are you fluent in Spanish?"

"Not fluent, but—"

"But, wham, just like that, your boss decided to send you to Cartagena. Is that right?"

Her fingers were still linked with Matthew's. She wanted to pull them free. It felt wrong to have his hand on hers when his voice, and his eyes, had turned into those of a stranger.

"Don't take that tone with me," she said softly.

"I'm just trying to figure things out. I mean, hell, it's like you were Dorothy, caught up in that tornado, you know? The old, 'I guess this isn't Kansas anymore, Toto,' thing. D.C. one day. Cartagena the next. As Hamilton's personal assistant." His tone hardened. "Living in his big, expensive mausoleum in the hills."

"I'd worked for Douglas before, when he was on assignment in Washington."

"So, it wasn't a fluke. Hamilton put in a special request. He asked Washington to give you to him."

"Nobody 'gave' me to Douglas."

"Let's not dance around it, okay? Hamilton requested you."

Mia pulled her hand free. "What is this all about?"

"It's not anything but friendly conversation. I'm just trying to figure out how a woman stationed in D.C. ended up on a plum detail in Latin America."

"A plum detail?" She gave a sharp laugh. "Remember what you said about Colombia? It's beautiful, but it's terribly dangerous."

"Cartagena's a city on a coast where the main problem of the day is which club to visit at night."

Mia pushed back her chair and got to her feet. Matthew shot to his.

"Where are you going?"

His voice was cold. So was hers.

"I told you, I don't like your tone."

"And I don't like people thinking they can walk out on me."

She swung away and started toward the house. He went after her, caught her by the shoulder and spun her to face him.

"Is there something between you and Hamilton?"

"I answered that before."

"He thinks there is."

"I can't help what he thinks."

"You didn't sleep with him?"

Mia's chin lifted. "If I did, it wouldn't be any of your business."

His hand tightened on her shoulder. "It damned well would."

"No, it wouldn't. You and I spent a night together. That doesn't entitle you to ask me questions about who I've slept with."

Matthew stared at her. Her eyes flashed with rebellion; her chin was sharply angled. She was ticked off and she had every right to be.

She was right. Her past was her affair...but it killed him to think she'd been with a man like the colonel.

"You're right," he said roughly, gathering her tightly against him. "Your past isn't my business. But from now on, you so much as look at another man..."

His mouth came down on hers. She held back for a second and then she went up on her toes and wound her arms around his neck.

He thought of what he'd just told her, of the insanity of staking a claim on a woman he didn't even know.

And then he stopped thinking of anything but carrying her to a chaise longue in a secluded corner of the terrace, stripping them both of their clothes and burying himself inside her.

In the blistering heat of midday, they headed down a narrow trail that wove through a stand of white oaks, Matthew with a pack slung over his shoulder, Mia with a bottle of water dangling from a strap.

He wouldn't tell her where they were going, except to say that it was a special place and that it was beautiful. Still, when they stepped from the trees into a small, lush green clearing, she gasped with surprise.

"Oh," she whispered. "Oh, Matthew… You were right. It's wonderful."

"Yeah." He cleared his throat. "I figured you'd like it."

She stared around her, at the ring of trees that stood watch over the silken grass, at the frothy waterfall tumbling down the face of a cliff into a natural pool of deepest sapphire.

"It's like—it's like the Garden of Eden."

"It's peaceful," he said softly, "and untouched. The kind of place where you can feel safe from the world."

She looked at him, knowing instinctively that he'd given her a glimpse of himself he kept hidden from everyone else. He seemed to realize it because he flashed a quick, embarrassed smile, dropped the pack under a tree and yanked off his T-shirt.

"Okay," he said briskly, "last one in gets stuck with tonight's dinner dishes."

"You're going to swim in that water?"

Her look of disbelief made him laugh. "Sure."

"But—but what about snakes?"

Matthew kicked off his sandals. "What about 'em?"

"Matthew—"

"I haven't seen an anaconda yet."

Mia paled. "An anaconda?"

"Yeah. You know. Maybe twenty feet long, two feet around… Baby, I'm teasing you. No anacondas, no crocs, no gators. We're in the mountains. The Amazon's a long way from here."

"I haven't got a swimsuit."

He laughed, unzipped his denim shorts and stepped out of them. "It's called skinny-dipping."

Mia's gaze skimmed over her lover. What *he* was called, was spectacular. He was gorgeous. A hunk of pure masculinity. Those shoulders. That chest. That long, amazing body…

"Not fair."

Her eyes flew to his. "What?"

"You're looking me over." His voice was husky; his laughter had stopped. "But you're not giving me the same opportunity."

"Of course I— Oh."

"Exactly. I'm wearing skin. You're wearing clothes." Matthew closed the distance between them. "Let me help you undress, baby."

"I can do it."

"I can do it better."

He was right. Oh, yes, he could do it so much better.

The feel of his hands on her arms as he drew her cotton tank top over her head. The brush of his knuckles against her belly as he unzipped her shorts. The whisper of his mouth on her throat as he bent his head, reached behind her and undid the clasp of her bra.

"You're so beautiful." She looked up at him and he cupped her face in his hands. "So beautiful," he said, taking her mouth with his.

She kissed him back, her fingers curling into the thick, silky hair at the base of his neck, her naked breasts soft against his muscled chest.

He'd made love to her over and over and yet, she was ready for him again, her nipples beading, aching for his touch, the secret place between her thighs turning wet and hot.

And he was ready for her. The power of his erection against her belly was as much proof as the way his hands were moving over her.

Slowly she lifted herself to him. Moved her hips

against his, glorying in the way he caught his breath. He cupped her face again and kissed her hungrily.

"Witch," he said in a husky whisper.

Knowing he wanted her so badly was electrifying. She was inexperienced, but not foolish. She knew Matthew could have any woman he wanted…and he wanted her.

She laughed softly against his mouth. "Is that what I am?"

"You know you are."

She looped her arms around his neck. Lifted one leg and wrapped it around his. He groaned with need, and it made her feel incredibly powerful.

"Keep at this," he said, "I'm going to back you against a tree and take you right here."

His words, the roughness in his tone, thrilled her. "Do it," she said, her voice hoarse with excitement.

Everything about him changed. His eyes darkened, his mouth thinned. The underpinning of bone in his face stood out in stark relief. For one wild moment, Mia feared the man who had become her lover… The man she thought had come to kill her.

"Matthew?" she said unsteadily.

His hands clasped her shoulders. He lifted her to her toes and kissed her, his tongue plundering her mouth as he pushed her back against an enormous oak at the edge of the clearing.

"Matthew," she said again, "wait…"

Too late.

Her cry was lost in the sound of the waterfall as he drove into her. His first thrust lifted her to her toes; his second brought her to a stunning climax. But he was still moving, pumping deep into her womb, and she wound her arms tightly around him, wrapped her legs around him as he cupped her bottom and took her soaring into the heavens with him, so hard, so fast she could only sob with pleasure as she came again and again and again.

His face contorted; a hoarse cry was wrung from his throat, and he exploded inside her.

They clung to each other for long seconds, bodies slippery with sweat, lungs straining for air. Then Matthew shuddered and gathered Mia tightly against him.

"Baby," he said softly, "sweetheart, I'm sorry."

She shook her head. "No. Oh, no. Don't be."

"Did I hurt you? God knows I didn't mean to. I just—"

"You didn't hurt me. That was—it was—"

"Wonderful."

"Yes."

He clasped her face in his hands, looked into her eyes and kissed her. She kissed him back and then she lay her head against his chest.

"I never—I never knew—"

"No," he said simply, "neither did I."

He held her close until he felt her heart, and his, stop racing. Then he drew back again and looked down at her. Her hair was tangled; bits of leaf clung to her skin. Her face was shiny, her mouth bruised from his kisses...

The feathery wings began beating in his chest again.

"Mia," he said, "Mia, I—I—"

"What?" she said, and waited. The forest seemed to wait with her, all the creatures that lived in it poised to hear words neither she nor he could possibly be crazy enough to feel or say.

"I'm glad I found you."

She lifted her eyes to his. "I'm glad you found me, too," she said softly.

He felt his heart swell. He kissed her, kissed her again and then, maybe because there was more to say and he wasn't ready to say it, he scooped her into his arms and flashed a wicked grin.

"Bath time," he said.

Mia's eyes widened. "No. Matthew, it'll be cold!"

"Ready or not," he said, and ran straight into the water. Laughing, he carried her deeper while she kicked and shrieked and laughed enough to make him wish he could freeze this moment and keep it, forever.

"Mia," he said, "Mia…"

Her laughter faded. So did his.

"Matthew," she whispered, and kissed him.

His mouth was a hot contrast to the chill of the pool, his body was hard and strong against hers…

And she finally knew there was no sense lying to herself.

Somewhere between yesterday and today, she'd fallen in love with Matthew Knight.

CHAPTER NINE

DAYS AND NIGHTS flowed one into another.

There were no clocks to watch, no outside world to observe them, no rules to obey.

The lovers laughed and talked; they feasted on the meals Evalina prepared and left for them, drank the wines stored in the cellar. They swam in the Olympic-size pool behind the house and luxuriated in the heated spa on the deck.

They took long walks through the cool woods and drove the narrow roads that wound through the mountains. They played Monopoly and Scrabble and watched really bad horror movies late at night, via satellite.

That is, they did those things when they weren't making love.

"Do you like this?" Matthew would say, bending his head to Mia's breasts. "This?" he'd whisper, parting her thighs. "And this?" he'd ask huskily, sliding deep inside her.

Her sighs, her moans, the swift clenching of her muscles as she closed around him, told him everything he needed to know.

Everything except the real reason she'd run from Cartagena.

He knew her, now. She was beautiful and feminine; walking toward him, naked, as she rose from the pool in the forest, she might have been painted by Botticelli.

But she was strong in all the ways that mattered.

He couldn't see her running from Hamilton, no matter how unwanted the man's attentions. She'd have looked the bastard straight in the eye and told him what she thought of him, but run?

The more Matthew knew Mia, the less likely that seemed.

But he'd given up asking her to tell him the truth. It hurt him that she wouldn't but he figured she had a damned good reason for it. When she was ready, he told himself, she'd share it with him.

In the meantime, they were on a voyage of sensual discovery.

Mia, uninhibited in her responses to his lovemaking, was, at first, reserved in her exploration of his body.

"Tell me what pleases you," she'd whisper, and he'd say she was what pleased him.

It was true. Just watching her comb her hair or step into the bath was enough to make him hard.

"Tell me," she'd insist.

"Touch me and find out," he finally said, with a little smile.

And, sweet Jesus, she did.

One night, on the terrace, with only the moon to see by, she undressed for him. She wouldn't let him help, wouldn't let him touch her.

She did it by herself, slowly, slowly, with all the

innate skill of Eve. By the time the last of her clothing drifted to the tile floor, he was half out of his mind.

He started to pull off his shirt. Mia stopped him.

"My job," she said softly.

She stripped away his shirt. His jeans. He had nothing on under them and when he sprang free, into her hands, he had to clench his teeth to keep from ending it right then.

"Is this for me?" she purred.

And then she drove him to the edge. Stroked him. Tasted him. Lowered herself onto his straining shaft while she watched his face. She rode him, her head back, her eyes closed in ecstasy, and he let her think she was in control until, with a primitive growl, he rolled her beneath him, pinned her arms above her head and drove her to the thin edge of release again and again, until she wept and begged for mercy.

"Please," she whispered. "Matthew, please…"

He let go of her wrists. Caught her face and kissed her mouth. Then he rose above her again and drove deep as she screamed his name into the night.

He collapsed on her. He knew he was too big, too heavy, but he couldn't move, didn't want to move.

Mia didn't want him to move, either. When he finally stirred, she held him tight.

"Stay," she whispered.

He kissed her mouth, her eyes, her throat. Then he rolled onto his back, tucked her into the curve of his shoulder, and held her close against his heart.

Mia sighed, shut her eyes and drifted to sleep.

Matthew watched the fire of the starry night wheel overhead, the fat moon drop from the sky. The past days and nights had changed him. Years ago, a woman he'd been involved with had grown angry at what she called his "removal." He was, she'd said angrily, a lone wolf.

It was the truth. Except for his brothers, he'd always been most content to be alone. Not anymore. He was most content, hell, he was only happy when he was with Mia.

What did that mean?

What did it mean? Matthew thought, and refused to reach for the word.

Another long, perfect day.

They drove to a little town high in the Andes where you could stroll across the street and step into Brazil. They ate tortillas and empanadas, drank icy cold beer and shared an ice-cream cone.

He bought her a corn-husk doll. She bought him a fetish hung from a leather cord.

It was, the vendor said, a bit of bone from the bravest of creatures. An eagle.

"An eagle for a man who wears an eagle," Mia said softly, as she slipped the leather cord over Matthew's head.

To her delight, he blushed.

"Did you really think I hadn't noticed your tattoo?" she said, smiling up at him. "He's beautiful. Just like you."

Matthew's blush deepened. "You're gonna pay for all this," he said, which delighted her even more.

"I hope so."

The look on his face made her laugh. She took his arm as they began walking again. "Did you get the tattoo when you were in the service?"

"In the…?" A muscle in his arm jerked under her hand. "When I was a soldier, you mean? No. Before that. It was a kid thing. I have two brothers."

How little she knew about her lover. "Older? Younger?"

"Older. We were born a year apart and we've always been close. Anyway, we all got a little, uh, a little stupid the night before Cam—he's the oldest—the night before he left for college."

"Meaning, you realized you were going to be separated, probably for the first time, and it upset you." She nuzzled his shoulder. "I think that's sweet."

Matthew grinned. "The truth is, we were drunk as skunks. All of a sudden, some memento, something we could share, seemed right. So we drove to this little place Cam had heard of, spent a while arguing over whether we should get tattoos of an eagle or a skull and crossbones…"

Mia gave a dramatic shudder. "I'm glad the eagle won."

"Yeah," he said, smiling. "Me, too. Anyway, it was just kid stuff."

"It was nice stuff," she said softly, hugging his arm.

"You think?" he said, and felt foolish because he couldn't stop the pleased grin that spread over his face.

"I know. I was an only child. I'd have given anything for brothers or sisters." She looked up at him and batted her lashes. "Besides…that eagle is very sexy."

"You're what's sexy," Matthew said, and kissed her right there, on the street, for all the world to see.

A shop caught Mia's eye. Matthew saw the way she gazed at a pale apricot dress in the window.

"Let's go inside and take a closer look," he said.

She shook her head. This wasn't a tourist shop. Everything here would be expensive.

"No," she said, "it's lovely, but—"

Matthew caught her hand and tugged her through the door. A smiling woman bustled toward them.

"Buenos dias."

"Buenos dias, señora. Quieremos comprar un vestido, el del aprador de la vitrina."

"No!" Mia gave the woman a quick smile, then turned to Matthew. "I don't want to buy the dress," she whispered. "It's too expensive."

"I want to buy it," he said softly.

"I can't let you."

"Aha," he said. "Discrimination!" His expression was serious, but his eyes laughed at her. "Ice cream's okay but a dress isn't."

"Matthew." Mia tried not to smile. "That's silly."

"She discriminates, and now she slanders me." He turned toward the shop's owner, who was watching the byplay and grinning. "What is a man supposed to do with a woman like this, *señora?* Unless…" He looked at Mia. "Unless, you don't like the dress."

"Of course I like it. It's beautiful. But—"

"Or you think it's not your size. Actually it does look kind of small."

"It's not too small."

"You sure?"

"Honestly, Matthew…"

"Honestly, Mia," he said gently, "I'm going to buy the dress." He put his hands on her waist and drew her toward him; the *señora* smiled and busied herself at a counter filled with brightly-colored silk scarves. "I want to see you in it," he said huskily. "And then I want to take you out of it. All those tiny buttons…"

Her eyes darkened, the way they always did when they made love. He bent his head and kissed her. Then he drew back, watched as her lashes slowly lifted and her eyes met his.

Mine, he thought, with sudden ferocity. *Mine, forever.*

The breath caught in his throat as he realized that the impossible had happened.

He was deeply, passionately in love.

Mia changed in the dressing room.

The dress was beautiful. She'd never owned anything like it. The neckline swooped low, showing the curve of her breasts. Her gaze fell to the little buttons that went all the way to the hem and she shuddered with pleasure, imagining Matthew undoing them, one by one.

There was a knock at the door. It opened just enough for a large, masculine hand to reach around the edge. Delicate accessories tumbled on the cool tile. Slender-heeled sandals that might have been spun of gold. A gold purse. A black lace *mantilla* that looked too fragile to be real.

Mia's heart turned over.

The emotions that filled her felt the same way. Too fragile to be real.

She leaned her forehead against the door. "Matthew," she said in a choked whisper, "really, I can't—"

"We're having dinner at a restaurant the *señora* assures me is deserving of all this elegance." She could hear the smile in his voice. "How can we disappoint her?"

How, indeed?

The *señora* was right.

The restaurant was perfect. It was small and candle-lit; a group of musicians played softly in the background. Their corner table offered a view shared only by an Andean condor, soaring on enormous wings a thousand feet over the mountains.

And yet, the only sight Matthew feasted his eyes on was Mia.

He'd been right about the pale apricot dress. It might have been made for her. Her skin, her eyes, her hair, streaming in loose curls over her shoulders, all seemed shot with gold.

He ordered for them both, steaks and *ensalada* and a bottle of Chilean cabernet sauvignon. Mia said everything was wonderful and he believed her, but he couldn't taste anything himself.

Mia filled his senses.

He loved her. God, he loved her.

And what in hell was he going to do about it?

Did a man tell a woman he loved her when she carried a secret she refused to share with him? Because the truth was, he knew, in his gut, that what Mia had told him about leaving Hamilton was a lie.

She hadn't left because he wouldn't take no for an answer. There was more to it than that.

Why wouldn't she let him know what it was? It killed him that she didn't trust him enough…but who was he to sit in judgment?

He had his own secrets.

He'd told her he'd been a soldier. Okay. He had, but there was more to it than that. He'd been a spy. A spook. Hell, he'd been an agent for a faceless government agency and even though he'd believed in his country, there were times he'd done things…

How would she feel, if she knew he had a past that still haunted him? If she knew that he'd been unable to save Alita, or even to avenge her death?

So many questions. So few answers. And yet, only one mattered. When he told Mia he loved her, would she tell him she loved him, too?

He reached across the table for her hand. The truth about himself, first. He'd tell her now. Right now.

"Mia?"

"Yes?"

Her eyes met his. He'd never seen her look happier. He was a man who prided himself on his courage but now, he felt his throat go dry.

"Mia," he said, and pushed back his chair. "Baby, will you dance with me?"

She went into his arms as if she'd been there all her life. As if she'd be there forever. And she would be, he thought, closing his eyes as he gathered her close. She would be his, always.

He touched his lips to her hair.

"Happy?" he said softly.

Mia nodded. She was almost afraid to speak. It was silly, she knew, but she could feel the tears gathering behind her eyes.

How come women cried when they were happy?

How could her terrifying flight from Cartagena have led to such bliss?

They were questions without answers, but so what? All that mattered was this. Being in Matthew's arms. Knowing she loved him.

Knowing she trusted him.

Because she did. No matter what she'd believed about him initially, she trusted him now.

It was time to tell him the truth. Everything, from start to finish.

That she worked for a faceless place known as the

Agency, even if she hadn't even heard of it a year ago and knew she'd never, ever want to work for them again.

That she'd been sent to Cartagena as Hamilton's P.A. so she could find out if he had turned and was working for the Rosario cartel.

Douglas grew suspicious. Without admitting anything, he'd accused her of spying on him. She denied it, and he decided to take out what he called "insurance."

He set it up to look as if she'd tried to smuggle cocaine to the States. Then he quashed the supposed attempt.

"Do anything stupid, and I'll turn you over to the local authorities," he'd said with a nasty smile. "Imagine how it will be to spend a few years in a Colombian prison."

And he made it equally clear that part of the price she'd pay for staying out of prison was warming his bed.

That was when she'd decided to run.

She'd found a list of Douglas's cartel contacts and the monies they'd paid him hidden on his computer. She downloaded the list to a mini compact disk and fled.

If she could just get to Bogotá, she'd told herself, get to the Embassy…

Except, Matthew intercepted her. And even though Douglas had sent him to find her, she'd come to trust him.

To trust him…

"Matthew," she said breathlessly. Couples around them were swaying to the music but Mia came to a stop. "Matthew." Her heart thudded as she looked up into the eyes of her lover. "I have to talk to you."

She saw, immediately, that he understood. She didn't want to discuss the weather or the wine or the food. She wanted to discuss what had brought them together…and what kept them apart.

He nodded. "That's good," he said, "because there are things I have to tell you, too."

He led her back to their table. She drew the mantilla around her shoulders and picked up her purse while he took a stack of bills from his wallet and left them for the waiter.

Then he led her out into the night.

They drove in silence, hands clasped on the console.

When they got to the house, Matthew stepped from the Escalade, went to the passenger side and helped Mia down. His hands lingered at her hips; he bent his head and they shared a long, tender kiss.

The moon hung over the forest; it lay an ivory path through the trees, to the clearing, the sapphire pool, the waterfall. To the place that belonged only to them.

The night was hushed. Expectant. Even the creatures that hunted in these dark hours were still.

When they reached the clearing, Matthew turned Mia toward him.

"Mia," he said softly.

No, she thought suddenly, not yet, and she put her hand lightly against his lips.

"You said you wanted to see me in this dress," she whispered. "Now it's time to see me out of it."

His eyes darkened. He said her name, drew her to him and kissed her, gently at first, then more and more urgently. She kissed him back that same way, as if both of them feared what might lie ahead.

Slowly, one by one, he undid the buttons of the apricot dress. When it fell at her feet, he felt his heart swell.

Mia smiled.

"It was a secret," she murmured, "between the *señora* and me."

Her bra was made of sheer lace, the same color as the dress. So was her thong. Against her golden skin, under the tender light of the moon, she might have been a gift to him from the ancient gods.

Matthew kissed her mouth. The long column of her throat. He kissed the swell of her breasts as he undid the clasp of the bra. Then he cupped her breasts, kissed her nipples, teased them into aching buds with his tongue and teeth.

Mia reached for him. Pushed his pale gray jacket from his shoulders. Undid the buttons of his shirt.

He was beautiful, all hard muscle and tanned skin. She kissed his lips, his shoulder, his chest. Skimmed her hands across his taut biceps and down his flat belly. He caught her wrist.

"Mia," he said roughly, "you're everything to me. I want you to know that. No matter what happens next."

She rose on her toes and kissed him. Then she slid her hand down under his waistband, wrapped it around all that hardness and heat, and he crushed her mouth beneath his.

The time for talking was past. Matthew stripped off the rest of his clothing, peeled the silk thong down her legs.

His name was on her lips as he took her down with him into the soft grass, then changed to a cry of wonder as he penetrated her.

"Matthew," she whispered, rising to him. Moving with him. Meeting him, thrust for thrust, until she cried out again, until his face contorted and his head fell back and he came in a hot, endless rush, filling her womb...

Filling her heart.

* * *

Long minutes later, lying in Matthew's arms, Mia sighed.

"You were right about this place," she said softly. "I feel safe here. I wish we never had to leave it."

It was the first admission either of them had made that they'd stolen these days from the fabric of time.

Matthew dropped a kiss on her forehead.

"This clearing will always belong to us, baby. Wherever we are, whatever happens, just close your eyes and you'll be here again."

Was that true? All at once, Mia had the feeling she'd never see this forest clearing again. She shivered, despite the warmth of the night, and Matthew's arms tightened around her.

"What is it, baby?"

"Nothing," she said quickly. "I'm just—I'm feeling chilly, that's all."

"Come on. I'll build a fire in the fireplace, we'll have some brandy—"

"And we'll talk."

He nodded. "Yes."

"Because—because I have to tell you the truth, Matthew. About—about Douglas and me."

"As soon as we get home."

They put their clothes on. Then Matthew put his arm around Mia's shoulders and drew her to his side as they walked along the moonlit path to the house.

But his smile was forced.

She had to tell him the truth, she'd said. About herself and Hamilton.

Why did that sound so ominous?

CHAPTER TEN

MIA STUMBLED as they climbed the steps to the deck. Matthew's encircling arm kept her from falling.

"You okay?"

"Fine. My heel caught, that's all." She smiled up at him. "I guess I'm not used to such high heels."

Matthew grinned. "Yeah," he said, "aren't they great?"

She laughed softly as he kissed her and she thought, for no reason whatsoever, *This is the last time you'll ever stand here, laughing over something silly with the man you love...*

"Here. Let me undo those straps and—"

"I'll do it. You go ahead and start the fire."

"You sure?"

"Positive." She touched her hand to his face, feeling the roughness of the end-of-day stubble on his jaw, remembering how she loved the feel of it against her breasts. "Matthew..."

"Yes?"

I love you. Suddenly she was afraid to say the words.

"What is it, sweetheart?"

"Nothing," she said brightly. "Just light the fire and pour us some brandy. I'll only be a minute."

He kissed her, a long, sweet kiss that tasted of the night and of him. Then he unlocked the sliding doors and went inside.

She knew what he was doing now. Punching in the code that would deactivate the security system, shrugging off his jacket, walking to the fireplace...

"Hello, Mia."

A hand clapped over her mouth, catching the scream in her throat. *Douglas. It was Douglas. He was here, he was here, he was here.*

"No noise," he said, his lips against her ear. His hand clamped down harder; her head tilted back under the pressure of it. "Not a sound, do you understand?"

She nodded. Douglas lifted his hand. Slowly Mia turned to face him.

"How are you, dear girl?" His lips curved in a cold smile. "No need to answer. I can see how you've been. You have the look of the happy whore all over you."

"Douglas—"

She gasped as he caught her chin in his hand and dug his fingers into her flesh.

"What did I tell you?" he whispered. "I'll do the talking. You'll just nod your head." His hand dropped to his side. "Now, dear girl, here's what we're going to do."

"Mia?"

"Answer him," Douglas hissed. Something hard and metallic jammed beneath the swell of her breasts. "Sound as if everything's fine or so help me..."

"In a minute, Matthew."

"The fire's lit, sweetheart. I'm pouring the brandy."

"I'll be right there."

"Sweetheart," Douglas purred. "How charming." The barrel of the gun dug in harder. "Looks as if the fearless

Mr. Knight will do anything for you, dear girl. The question is, will you do anything for him?"

"Douglas. Please, I beg you—"

"You're coming back to Cartagena with me."

"No!"

"You're going to tell him that it's your idea. That you and I had a lovers' quarrel but it's over now and you're thrilled I came for you." The barrel of the gun moved to her breast. "Do it," Hamilton growled, "and make it believable, or I'll kill him. I'll shoot him first, while you watch, dear girl, and there won't be a thing you can do to help him. Understand?"

Mia bit back a sob.

"Is that a yes?"

"Yes," she whispered.

"Excellent. Oh, and just in case you think he might have a chance against me… I'm not alone. Two of Rosario's men are out there, in the darkness. Anything goes wrong in this little drama, they'll handle things. Got that?"

She got it, and fully believed it. The cartel's men were stone-cold killers, and so was Hamilton. The disk still secreted in her compact held all the proof of that.

The deck lights blazed on. Hamilton slid his arm around her. His hand, slipped casually into his jacket pocket, gripped his gun.

The doors slid open. Matthew stepped onto the deck…and went rigid with shock.

Hamilton? Here? He couldn't believe it. Nobody but his brothers knew about this place.

"Good evening, Mr. Knight. How nice to see you again."

And why was Mia standing so close to the man she'd run from? Why was his arm around her?

Matthew tore his eyes from her and glared at the colonel.

"What are you doing here?"

The colonel smiled. "I don't suppose you'd buy the story that I happened to be in the neighborhood... No. I didn't think so."

"Get the hell off my property."

"Come now, Mr. Knight. Here we are, fellow Americans on foreign soil. I should think you'd be more hospitable, especially to the man who hired you."

"You didn't hire me. There's no money involved here."

"Correct, Mr. Knight. However, you did agree to find Mia—and here she is."

"Mia?" Matthew looked at the woman he loved. She was pale. What a shock for her, to find Hamilton here. "Mia," he said softly, holding out his hand, "come to me, baby."

"She's quite happy where she is, Mr. Knight. Aren't you, darling? Ah. Well, she won't answer. She's asked me to handle this. Understandable, when you think of how cozy she's made you feel."

"Mia," Matthew said sharply. "Step away from him. Now."

"I don't like hearing you give orders to my fiancée, Mr. Knight."

"She isn't your fiancée."

"Is that what she told you?" The colonel shook his head. "Mia, Mia, why must you play these games?"

"Douglas." Mia's voice shook. "Douglas, please—"

"Hamilton," Matthew said sharply. "Let go of her. Now."

The colonel raised his eyebrows. "Really, Mr. Knight—"

"Now," Matthew barked.

Hamilton shrugged. One last nudge of the gun and he stepped away from Mia.

"Certainly, if that's what you prefer. But I'm afraid it won't change anything. Mia understands the situation. Don't you, dear girl?"

Mia nodded. Yes. She understood. Hamilton's hand was in his pocket, clamped around the grip of his gun. Somewhere in the blackness beyond the deck, two men who killed as much for pleasure as for purpose had their weapons trained on the man she loved.

The man whose life she could only save by breaking her heart, and his.

"Mia," Matthew said, his eyes locked to hers. "Come to me. I'll protect you."

"There's nothing to protect me from," she said carefully. "I'm fine, Matthew. I know that's hard for you to believe but really, I'm all right."

His eyes narrowed. She knew he was telling himself she was lying, maybe even coming up with the actual reason for it. She couldn't let him do that. Maybe he had a chance against Douglas, but the men beyond the deck would shoot him in an instant.

Mia took a deep breath, stepped closer to the colonel and forced herself to slide her arm through his.

"Mia." Matthew's voice was rough. "What the hell are you doing?"

"I—I—" The look on his face was tearing her apart. "Matthew, I—"

"It's all right, dear girl," the colonel said. "I'll handle this for you. You see, Knight, I'd hoped we could meet alone. Two men of the world, discussing a problem, without Mia's presence to complicate things."

"Fine. Let's do that," Matthew said, his eyes never leaving Mia. "Get off my property and phone for an appointment."

"I have. Several times." Hamilton smiled again, this time with a feral show of teeth. "You don't seem to have been monitoring your messages. But I understand. Miss Palmieri can be a great diversion. I suppose that's the reason you're showing me such hostility. That's no way for a government operative to act."

Mia gasped. "What?"

"He's lying. I used to work for them but I don't, not anymore. Goddammit, Hamilton, what's going on here?"

"He's right. He doesn't work for them anymore." Hamilton chuckled. "He does freelance work now, for the highest bidder. You know. Checks out difficult situations. Finds ways to get the goods on those the people who hire him don't trust." A short pause, and then his voice turned hard. "People like you, Mia."

"He's lying, damn it! He asked me to find you! I don't have a damned thing to do with the government. Mia? Damn it, talk to me!"

"Let me explain for you, dear girl. You see, Mr. Knight, Mia came to Cartagena as my P.A. but she was much more than that. We'd fallen in love, in Washington, and wanted to be together."

"Mia?" Matthew said, and she knew she'd remember the despair in his voice as long as she lived.

"But our girl decided to take a walk on the wild side. The drug smuggling via the embassy pouch? All true, I'm afraid. As my P.A., she had the access and cover. Unfortunately for her, I discovered what she'd done. I felt sorry for her and, well, I said I wouldn't turn her in if she'd go back to the States immediately."

Matthew, Mia thought, *oh Matthew, my love…*

"I'm ashamed to say, my trust was misplaced. She fled from my house with a list of every undercover federal agent in Cartagena. I had to get her back, but I couldn't tell anyone."

"Not without implicating yourself in the cover-up you engineered for her."

Hamilton nodded. "Exactly."

Matthew turned to Mia. "Tell me he's lying."

"Yes, dear girl," Hamilton said smoothly. "Tell him what he wants to hear—and the consequences be damned."

The warning was clear. Hamilton had woven a monstrous lie, based on an underpinning of truth. Mia drew a deep breath.

"I can't—I can't tell you that, Matthew."

"You tried to smuggle cocaine?"

All she could manage was a whispered "yes."

"You stole a list of undercover agents. You were ready to turn them over to people who'd kill them?" He rushed toward her and caught her by the elbows. Eyes black with rage, he hoisted her to her toes. "And you were this—this pig's woman?"

She didn't answer, but she knew Matthew would take her silence as a yes.

His hands tightened on her until she thought her bones might shatter.

"And you slept with me because?" His mouth thinned. "Hell, don't bother trying to come up with an answer. I know what it is. Sleeping with me kept me in line. It kept me from contacting Hamilton. From seeing to it that you went back to face the music."

"Sad but true, I'm afraid," Hamilton said in stentorian tones. "She's very good at getting men to do her bidding."

Matthew ignored him. "One last chance," he said to Mia, softly, as if they were alone. "It's not too late. Tell me it wasn't a lie. Everything you did in my bed, everything we shared…" Anguish mixed with the fury blazing in his eyes. "Tell me he's the one who's lying. Say it, and I'll believe you."

Mia wanted to put her arms around him. To lift her mouth to his, kiss him and tell him she loved him, she adored him, she would love him until the end of time…

"Say it, damn you," he roared.

She didn't answer. His eyes went flat and cold; he took his hands from her with exaggerated care and stepped back. The man she'd fallen in love with was gone, replaced by the dangerous stranger who'd abducted her from her hotel room days before.

"What now?"

The question was directed at Hamilton. The colonel sighed.

"I'll take her to Cartagena. She'll return what she stole and she'll behave herself from now on or, this time, I *will* tell my superiors, even though it means I'll probably be court-martialed for covering for her." He paused. "I'm sorry about this, Knight. I should have realized Mia would… She's the type of woman who just can't seem to keep from… Well. Never mind. Mia? I assume you have that list of agents with you?" At her nod, the colonel wrapped a hand around her wrist and held out the other to Matthew. "Goodbye, Mr. Knight. Thank you for your help."

Matthew looked at the extended hand, then deliberately put his own hands in his trouser pockets.

"Get the hell off my property, Colonel," he repeated in a soft, deadly voice. "If I ever see you again, you're a dead man."

Mia felt Hamilton's fury in the way he tightened his grip on her wrist, but his voice gave nothing away.

"Come, dear girl. We've given Mr. Knight a difficult time. Let us permit him to sulk in private."

Her feet wouldn't move. Hamilton all but dragged her to the steps, then down them to the ground.

"Matthew," she said in a broken whisper. Hamilton clasped her more tightly but she turned and shot her lover a last look. "The same as choosing the skull and crossbones over the eagle… The end always justifies the means."

"One more word," Hamilton hissed, "and you'll sign his death warrant."

It didn't matter. Her pathetic attempt at warning Matthew that Hamilton had forced her to go with him was a failure. Matthew had already turned his back and walked to the far end of the deck.

He was lost to her, forever.

The colonel half-dragged her around the house, to where his car and driver waited. Once there, he bound her hands and shoved her into the back seat, then got in beside her.

The driver gunned the engine and the car sped up the road.

Mia craned her neck, trying to see out the rear window.

"The men with you," she said desperately. "Call them off."

Hamilton chuckled. "Wasn't that an excellent story? I'm delighted you believed it." He leaned close to her.

"I can hardly wait to get you home again, dear girl. What fun we're going to have together."

She didn't think. She acted, and spat full into his face. Hamilton snarled and backhanded her across the mouth but it didn't matter.

Nothing mattered, now.

Nothing ever would, without Matthew.

The sound of the car engine faded and silence returned to the forest.

Matthew stood on the deck, unmoving, staring into the dark night while he cursed himself. And Hamilton. And the government...

And Mia.

How could he have been such a fool?

He knew how easily a man could misjudge things when he was operating under stress, how simply he could be diverted from the truth.

There were endless tricks of the trade in covert ops. Lies, fabrications, miscues. Double agents, men who'd look you in the eye and swear they were telling the truth.

Women schooled in the art of deceit. The art of the honey trap.

He clenched his fists. How could he have been such an easy target? He'd gone after Mia knowing exactly what she was but somehow or other, that reality had slipped his mind.

She was innocent, she'd said. And, pow, just like that, he'd believed her. She hadn't had to try very hard to convince him.

A few passionate kisses—a few nights in his bed, he thought coldly—and he'd done the convincing all by himself.

If there was any small comfort in all of this, it was that he hadn't made a complete fool of himself tonight. What if he'd told her that he loved her? Just imagine if he'd stood on this deck, taken her in his arms and said, *Mia, I love you.*

Except, he wouldn't have done that.

He'd have come to his senses in plenty of time because the truth was, he didn't love her and never had. Thinking he loved her had been a lie he'd told himself.

Maybe it had to do with the way they'd met. He as the hunter, she as his prey. There was something sexy in that, wasn't there?

Or maybe it was the way she'd trembled in his arms. How she'd lifted her face to his when he kissed her...

Matthew gripped the deck railing.

What the hell did it matter? It was over. Done. Finished, and to hell with standing around feeling sorry for himself.

He spun on his heel, went into the house, picked up the pair of Baccarat brandy snifters and went to the sideboard.

What he'd felt for Mia was lust. Lust...

"Goddammit!"

His face contorted. He pivoted toward the fireplace and slung the glasses into the flames. Then he grabbed the bottle of brandy and took a long swallow.

He thought of all he should have said before letting her leave. How sleeping with her hadn't meant anything to him. How he'd slept with a dozen other women who'd been better in bed than she could ever hope to be.

How holding her in his arms through the long nights had just been part of the game.

He took another drink.

It had all been a game. For her and for him. And that

was okay. It was fine. Hell, after a while, it might even make for a good story. How the hotshot ex-operative had spent a wild couple of weeks in Colombia, screwing a woman who'd turned out to be operating him.

One more shot of brandy. And then another and another until the bottle was half-empty. Then he killed the fire. Grabbed his jacket. Made sure he had his keys, his wallet, his passport.

"Time to go home," he said to the silent house.

Time to go back to his life.

To Dallas.

CHAPTER ELEVEN

IT WAS AMAZING, the things that money could buy.

Matthew was rich.

He never thought of himself that way. He'd grown up rich, but that money was his father's. He hadn't wanted any part of it.

Risk Management Specialists had made him wealthy in his own right, but he never really thought about it. He'd bought a bi-level condo in Turtle Creek and a Ferrari. He lived well, traveled well, bought things that caught his fancy, gave the women he dated expensive gifts.

Now, for the first time, he knew what money could do.

It made it possible to put a piece of your life behind you.

He drove out of the valley, heading for a small, private airport, tearing along the narrow roads at speeds that would have been foolish even if he hadn't drunk all that brandy, but he didn't give a damn.

The night, the fast-moving clouds, the sharp drop-off to his right, all suited his mood.

The truth was, he didn't much care what happened next.

It was the way he'd started feeling just before he left

the Agency, that I-don't-give-a-crap state of mind that he knew was dangerous as hell—and couldn't prevent.

He'd always survived those black moments in the past and he'd survive this one, too.

It was close to midnight by the time he pulled into the airport. It was unstaffed—he'd figured as much—but there was a telephone number posted on the gate. For Emergencies, it said in English and Spanish.

Matthew decided that's what this damned well was, and took his cell phone from his pocket.

A couple of calls, and he was talking to a sleepy-voiced guy who owned a Learjet 60. *Si,* he could fly the *señor* to the States but no, he could not do it now. It was impossible. He could not fly out of the Cachalú at night. The darkness, the mountains… It was too dangerous.

In the morning, and for the right fee…

"What's the right fee?" Matthew said.

The pilot hesitated. "Fifty thousand dollars American," he said.

Matthew didn't blink. "Fly me out now," he said, "and I'll double it."

An hour later, they were in the air.

Five hours after that, he wasn't home. He was in Houston.

His father answered the door himself.

Avery was unshaven and bleary-eyed but then, it was barely six in the morning. Matthew had phoned as the plane touched down, awakened his old man and announced that he'd be there in half an hour.

At that, he figured he'd been more than polite.

A man who sent you into an Agency-connected mess

without warning you first didn't deserve a lot in the way of good manners.

"Coffee?" Avery said. "I just made it."

Matthew nodded and followed his father into the kitchen. The coffee was strong and hot and he loaded his cup with sugar. A caffeine high, a sugar rush... He needed both.

"How was Cartagena?" his father said, sitting across from him at a marble-topped table.

The question of the year, Matthew thought, and smiled tightly.

"Hot."

"Yes, well... I assume you met with Douglas Hamilton?"

"Oh, I met with him, all right." Matthew narrowed his eyes. "Tell me, father, when you asked me to help him, did you know what kind of man he was?"

"What kind of—"

"Hamilton's a slimy son of a bitch."

"Is he? I've never met him. It's his father who was my friend."

"He wanted me to hunt down a woman." Matthew's jaw knotted. "His woman."

"That's what he wanted? I'm sorry, son. Had I known, I'd never have bothered you with it."

Matthew felt some of his anger fade. Avery's bewilderment couldn't have been faked.

And when had he ever heard the old man call him "son," or say he was sorry?

"Yeah, well, I found her."

"Then, why do you look so distressed?"

Matthew stared at his father. *None of your business,*

he started to say…but what came out was something entirely different.

"I got involved with her," he said quietly. "The whole thing got personal, and it shouldn't have."

Avery nodded. "Caring for a woman can complicate things."

"I didn't care for her," Matthew countered sharply. "I told you, I got involved, that's all. I just—I just—" His eyes met Avery's, then slid away. "I made a fool of myself, is what I did," he said. "Damn it, I should have known better!"

"You can't know better, when you fall in love."

"Father, I keep telling you—"

"It's what happened to me, when I met your mother."

Matthew's eyebrows lifted. He couldn't recall his father ever talking about his mother before.

"I loved her so much that I was afraid to show it. Your mother changed my life and I guess I figured, if she ever stopped loving me…" Avery gave a self-deprecating laugh. "But she never did. Her love was the one constant in my world. When she died…when she died, I was lost. I poured myself into my work and—and I neglected you and your brothers. I regret it, to this day, but—"

"Yes," Matthew said bluntly. "You did." His voice softened. "But—but I'm glad you told me the reason. I mean, I can understand how losing her must have—must have devastated you…" He cleared his throat. "This isn't the same. This woman—she didn't love me. And I didn't love her."

Avery nodded. "Of course not," he said softly.

Father and son sipped their coffee in companionable silence. Then Matthew sighed and rose to his feet.

"I've got to get to the office."

Avery walked him to the door. "With luck, son, you'll look back at this someday and find some good in it. Time teaches us lessons." He smiled. "You know. Don't cry over spilt milk, take things a day at a time…"

"Yeah." Matthew smiled, too. "And the end justifies the means."

Father and son looked at each other, then, a bit awkwardly, exchanged what might have passed for a hug. Then Matthew went down the walk and climbed into the taxi that had waited for him.

"The airport," he said, but what he kept thinking was what he'd just said to his father.

The end justifies the means.

Why would those words be rattling around in his head?

The flight to Dallas took less than an hour.

By midmorning, Matthew was at his desk, poring over the mail that had built up while he was gone…

Trying not to think about Mia. About Hamilton. About what he was doing with her, in that big house up in the hills overlooking Cartagena.

His brothers were in the office today, too. Unusual, Cam said, and it was. Generally, at least one of them was away on business.

At noon, Alex rang their intercoms. "How about lunch?"

"Fine," Cam said.

Matthew said he couldn't spare the time.

At one, it was Cam who suggested lunch.

Alex said yes. Matthew said he wasn't hungry.

At two, Alex and Cam huddled in the conference room. Matt didn't sound right, Cam muttered. Yeah, and he didn't look right, either, Alex added.

Something was up, but what?

Five minutes later, they walked into Matt's office.

"Lunch," Cam said firmly.

"Right now," Alex added, just as firmly.

Matthew looked at his brothers. They stood, one on either side of his desk, arms folded, jaws set.

He sighed.

"What's the deal here? We go for lunch, or I get to take on both of you?"

"See?" Alex grinned at Cam. "Told you he had a functional brain."

Cam jerked his thumb at the door. "Let's go."

Matthew thought about duking it out. A little physical action would probably improve his mood but his brothers, for all their swagger, looked worried.

He sighed again and pushed back his chair. "How'd you guys know I was getting hungry?"

They set out for a bar a few blocks away. It was a place where you could get a pretty good hamburger and a beer without stained glass hanging over your head or an asparagus fern dangling in your eye.

The brothers settled in their favorite booth and gave the waitress their order.

Alex commented on the weather. Cam commented on the traffic. Matthew made no comment at all.

Cam cleared his throat.

"So," he said, after exchanging a meaningful look with Alex, "how was Colombia?"

"Okay."

Silence. The waitress brought their beer. Cam raised an eyebrow at Alex. *Your turn, pal,* the raised eyebrow said.

Alex cleared his throat, too. "You take care of whatever it was the old man wanted done down there?"

Matthew raised his glass to his lips. "Uh-huh."

More silence. More looks flashing between Cam and Alex.

"Guess I'm the only one hasn't been asked to do a good deed for our esteemed *padre*," Alex said briskly.

"Give it time," Cam said.

"Yeah," Matthew said. "And when he finally asks, watch your ass."

Nine whole words, Cam thought. Almost a record for the day.

"Because?"

"Because, you might just want to be smart and say, no way. You need a job done, do it yourself."

"Well," Cam said carefully, "it worked out okay for me. I mean, if I hadn't said 'yes' to what the old man asked, I wouldn't have found Salome."

Matthew looked up from his beer. "You ended up in intensive care," he said coldly. "Anybody in his right mind would just as soon pass on that."

"What counts is that I met the woman I love."

There was tension in Cam's tone, almost a challenge, but Matthew ignored it.

"Yeah, well, the love crap—" He raised his hands in apology at the sudden flash of heat in Cam's eyes. "Sorry. I'm glad it's real for you, man. Hell, I'm crazy about my new sister-in-law. You know that. But that doesn't mean l-o-v-e isn't b.s. for ninety-nine percent of the rest of us."

Another long look passed between Alex and Cam.

"Are we, uh, are we talking about a particular woman?" Alex asked.

"Who said we were talking about a woman at all?"

"Well, nobody said it, but you said love was—"

"I know what I said. And no, we're not talking about a particular woman."

"Good. Good, because if we were—"

"Do I look like the kind of idiot who would fall for a woman and let her make a fool of me? Do I?"

Yes, both his brothers thought, because looking at him now, they could see a volatile mix of emotions in his eyes. Anger. Pain. Despair, and something else…

"No," Cam said slowly. "But, on the other hand, if maybe you ran into something, ah, something that shook you up, down in Colombia, well, you know, you might want to talk it out."

Matthew glared at him. "I may have behaved like an idiot but that doesn't mean I'm ready for group therapy."

"Of course not, but—"

"You think I'm somebody who'd curl up on a couch and spill my guts to a shrink?"

"No. Still—"

"Or maybe you think I'd fall for a babe I knew wasn't any damned good? A woman who tried smuggling drugs? Who belonged to another man? Is that what you think?" Matthew slammed his fist on the scarred wooden table. "Is it?" he snarled.

And before his brothers could answer, he told them the whole story.

Everything, from meeting Hamilton to chasing down Mia to falling crazy in love with her and finding out she'd played him for a fool.

Except, he didn't call it falling crazy in love.

He called it "being infatuated."

Alex breathed a sigh of relief.

"Okay. Got to tell you, man, for a little while there, you had us worried."

"Nothing to worry about," Matthew grumbled. "I just hate being played for a patsy."

"Yeah," Cam said, "but now that you told us the story, you'll be fine." He looked around, raised a hand to signal for another round. "All you had to do was get the details out in the open. I mean, a guy gets taken by a babe who's got the morals of an alley cat—"

Matthew was across the table before Cam finished the sentence, his hands clasping the lapels of his brother's suit jacket as he half-dragged him from his seat.

"What'd you say?"

"Matthew," Cam said slowly, his hands locking around Matthew's wrists, "don't do something we'll both regret."

"You made a comment about Mia, Cameron. I want to be sure I heard it right."

"Hey." Alex looked from one hard, angry face to the other. "C'mon, take it easy. Matt, you said some things that maybe we misunderstood. Cam, Matt's upset. We can all see that."

"I am not upset," Matthew said through his teeth… and then his mouth twisted, he looked from Cam to Alex and back again, let go of Cam's lapels and sank back in the booth. "Jesus," he whispered, "what the hell am I going to do?"

"You're in love with her," Cam said softly.

Matthew nodded. "And isn't that the saddest thing you ever heard?"

"Well—well, maybe things aren't as bad as they seemed. Maybe she's not—maybe she wasn't—"

"She was. Hell, she didn't even try to deny the things Hamilton said. He called her a thief, a smuggler. He said she'd stolen secret information she was going to sell, that she'd played me for a sucker…"

"And she didn't say anything?"

"No. She didn't string more than half a dozen words together, not until the end when she was leaving with him, and then what she said didn't make sense because it referred to something personal, about me."

"What?"

Matthew gave a bitter laugh. "To this dumb tattoo we all have, can you believe it? And she even got it wrong. She said, just like choosing the skull and crossbones over the eagle, the end always justifies the…" The color drained from his face. "Sweet Jesus," he whispered.

"Matthew?"

"She *knew* it was the other way 'round. We'd talked about it only a couple of hours earlier. She asked me about my tattoo and I told her how we'd debated whether to get a skull and crossbones or an eagle, and how the eagle had won, and she knew that. She *knew!*"

Cam and Alex exchanged bewildered looks.

"And?" Alex said.

"And," he said, his voice suddenly hoarse, "I was too busy wallowing in self-pity to get the message."

"Yeah, well, count us in because we don't get it, either."

"Mia loves me," Matthew said with conviction. "She's not the woman Hamilton said she was—and, dear God, I let that son of a bitch take her away!"

He shot to his feet, took out some bills and dropped them on the table. He was halfway to the door before his brothers caught up to him.

"What're you talking about?" Cam said.

"Yeah, man. You gonna let us in on the mystery?"

"It wasn't Mia who scammed me, it was Hamilton. And I—I fell for it. I let him take her with him." Matthew ran to the curb and flagged a taxi. "God only knows what he'll do to her. What he's already done to her."

"Matt. Wait a minute…"

Matthew jumped into the cab. It was a small vehicle. Any sane person would have said three men the size of the Knights couldn't possibly fit into the back seat, but they did.

The Learjet Matthew had chartered for his flight home was still at the airport. The pilot was just getting ready to make the return trip to Colombia.

"No problem," he said, when Matthew ran into the private aircraft terminal, yelling that he wanted to charter the Lear again.

The brothers scrambled on board. Matthew dug out his cell and punched in a number he'd never forgotten.

The same dispassionate voice from the past answered. Matthew gave the right code words. Seconds later, he was talking to the man known as the Director, who had run black ops for the Agency as long as anyone could remember.

When the conversation ended, his expression was grim.

"Son of a bitch," he said tonelessly. "I should have known. Nothing's changed. Black is always white and white is always black in the Agency's world."

"Mia wasn't running drugs?" Alex said.

"She was a secretary, working at the Department of Defense. A secretary, goddammit! But they didn't care. They got word Hamilton might be dirty, went through the files and learned she'd worked for him, called her in and handed her a load of b.s. about it being her patriotic duty to get the goods on him. Then they sent her down to Cartagena to be Hamilton's P.A."

"And she got the proof they wanted."

"Yes. He's the one. The turncoat. The smuggler. Mia got hold of the names of his contacts. That's why she ran, and why he had to get her back."

Cam cursed, softly and eloquently. "It's gonna take us, what, five, six hours to reach Cartagena."

"An eternity," Matthew said, his voice low and rough. "I told that to the Director. I told him what was happening and he said okay, he had enough to raid Hamilton's house."

"And?"

"He'll raid it…but not for another twenty-four hours. He says that's how long it'll take to coordinate the Agency, DEA and the Colombian cops."

"That's too long."

"You bet your ass it is." Matthew looked at his brothers. "I'm not Agency. I'm not DEA and I'm damned well not the cops. I'm gonna make a couple of calls, line up some gear."

Nobody asked what kind of gear he meant. They knew. Weapons. Wire cutters. Electronic stuff. Whatever would get them into Hamilton's place—and get Mia out.

"I can hit Hamilton almost as soon as we touch the ground." Matthew paused. "But I want you guys to turn right around and fly home. Having you with me now is great, but—"

"But," Alex said to Cam, "he doesn't want to let us in on the good stuff."

"Yeah," Cam said, "well, what can you expect? He always was a selfish little snot. Never would share things that were fun."

"Like his tricycle."

"Or his train set."

"And his blocks. Man, he never let me play with those."

Alex and Cam glared at Matthew. He glared back, and then his eyes turned suspiciously bright.

"You guys," he said, his voice rough and low, "you guys are—you're the—"

"The best," Cam said archly.

The brothers grinned. The grins faded, turned to the determined looks of hard, experienced men. Matthew sketched out a drawing of the colonel's house, then got busy on the phone.

Cam and Alex got busy on a plan.

CHAPTER TWELVE

HIS BROTHERS said if he continued pacing, Matthew would end up walking to Colombia.

He knew they were trying to lighten the tension, but the only thing that would do that was getting Mia back. He remembered the look on her face the last time he saw her, and it killed him to know he'd turned away from her when she'd needed him the most.

How could he have believed Hamilton? He should have known the truth, that Mia would never have done the things the colonel accused her of.

If she were dead...

No. He wasn't going there. She was alive. She had to be. He'd know if she weren't. He'd know.

An envelope had been left for Matthew at the service desk at the airport.

Inside was a parking receipt and the keys for an SUV. Another envelope that held a slip of paper with an address scrawled on it lay waiting in the truck's glove compartment.

Matthew drove; he knew the streets of Cartagena better than his brothers.

Moments later, he pulled up outside a ramshackle house in one of the city's most dangerous slums. A man let them in, someone Matthew had known years ago. They had no names for each other but friend.

"You gave me short notice," the man said in English. "I got what I could."

Uzis. Walthers. Berettas. Tiny communications devices. A pair of wire cutters. Half a dozen other tools, and a small vial of sleeping tablets and a half kilo of chopped steak. Black jeans, black turtlenecks, black ski masks and black running shoes for all three Knights.

The stuff would do.

Matthew and his brothers emptied their wallets of cash but, of course, it wasn't enough.

The man scooped up the pile of bills, smiled and pocketed it.

"Su credito es bueno, amigo," he said, and grinned.

It was an old joke between them, based on signs that hung in downscale shop windows in Cartagena as well as in some stores in Dallas, but the best Matthew could manage was a nod.

"Gracias, amigo."

And then, at last, they were on the road that led to Hamilton's house.

The plan was simple.

Simple plans almost always worked best.

They'd park half a mile from the house, wait until midnight—less than an hour away. They'd lure out the dog or dogs, drop sleeping-tablet laced lumps of chopped beef over the fence, scale the wall, cut the razor wire…

And then play things as they went.

At five minutes to twelve they left the SUV, approached the walled house by creeping through the scrub on the large, empty lot that adjoined it. When they reached the walls, Cam gave a soft whistle. Immediately they heard the padding hurry of animal feet.

"One dog," Alex whispered. "Big. A rotter, maybe, or a German shepherd."

Cam nodded, waited until the dog was at the wall, then hurled the bait across.

They heard snuffling, then munching. Then, after what seemed a very long time, the sound of an animal lying down, followed by its unmistakable snores.

"Let's move out," Matthew whispered.

Up the wall. Snip the razor wire. Drop noiselessly onto the soft grass on the other side. Hand signals were all they needed to communicate; they'd worked together many times in the past. Each knew the others' minds as well as his own.

There were half a dozen vehicles parked in front of the house.

Matthew narrowed his eyes. They'd hoped everyone would be asleep at this hour, but this looked as if a meeting were taking place. That made the odds tougher, but it also meant they might catch lots of fish.

He'd blanked his mind to thoughts of Mia. If he thought about her, he knew he'd be unable to function.

The brothers moved on his signal. Scaled the walls of the house. Entered through a window on the second floor. Checked all the rooms, found them empty. Began creeping down the service stairs, to the kitchen.

Alex clapped a hand, then a strip of duct tape over the cook's mouth. Cam secured her hands and feet with cord and whispered that they weren't going to hurt her if she behaved herself.

They slipped into the pantry. Listened at the door to the dining room, where a late meal was clearly in progress. Heard at least half a dozen voices, lots of laughter, lots of ribald jokes.

Matthew recognized Hamilton's voice...

And one other.

His skin crawled.

It was the voice of the man who'd gotten away after murdering Alita, the voice he'd heard in his nightmares all these years.

He took a deep breath. Signaled to Cam and Alex.

Weapons at the ready, the Knights burst into the dining room.

Six men, seated at the big dining room table. Six bodyguards, standing along one wall. The surprise was total. Then one of the bodyguards reached into his waistband.

It was over in seconds. Seconds that felt like hours, as they always did in times like this.

When it was over, three of the bodyguards were dead. Three were wounded. Of the men who'd sat at the table, two lay motionless on the floor. Four others still sat in their chairs, hands flat on the table top, faces white.

They were, indeed, big fish.

Juan Maria-Rosario, the head of the cartel.

Colonel Douglas Hamilton.

One of the biggest North American cocaine distributors.

And the unnamed man who'd escaped from Matthew after Alita's murder. The man looked at Matthew and turned white.

"You," he said.

Matthew smiled. "Me," he said softly.

The man eased back from the table. "Listen, man. It was nothing personal. Take it easy, okay? Let's talk this over—"

On the last word, he sprang from his chair, an automatic in his hand. But Matthew was quicker. He fired, and Alita's killer lay sprawled at his feet, dead.

Matthew gave the body a long look. *For you, Alita,* he thought, and felt a weight lift from his heart.

Cam was on his cell phone, calling the Director. Alex was tying up their prisoners. Matthew made straight for the colonel, grabbed him by the front of his shirt and hauled him to his feet.

"Where is she?"

Hamilton's face was white, his eyes bulging with fear. "Don't kill me. This is all a mis—"

Matthew dragged him to his toes. "Where is she?" he roared.

"I don't know."

Hamilton gagged as Matthew moved his hand from the colonel's shirt to his throat. "One last time, you sorry son of a bitch. Where's Mia, or so help me God—"

His brothers pulled him off.

"You kill him," Cam said matter-of-factly, "the world'll be better off... but you won't find Mia."

Matthew dragged in a breath. Cam was right. He nodded, took a step back, waited until Hamilton was bound, hand and foot.

"Now," he growled, "where is Mia?"

The colonel shook his head. "I don't know."

"Liar!"

"No. No, it's true. She's not here. Search the house. You'll see for yourself. She isn't here."

That much was true. They'd searched the upper floor.

Now, Alex came into the dining room and shook his head. Mia wasn't on this level, either.

"Then—then, she's dead," Matthew said tonelessly. "You had her taken out into the jungle and—"

"No! I didn't. Mia—Mia's gone. She didn't want to stay with me."

"What?"

"I said, she came home with me but—but she changed her—"

Hamilton gasped as Matthew sprang at him and wrapped his hands around his throat.

"Liar! She didn't come with you. You forced her."

"You know better than that, Knight. You know what she's like. She plays games. She—"

He cried out as Matthew's thumbs pressed into his Adam's apple. "She was working for the Agency."

"All right. Yes, she was. But she turned. I told you that."

Matthew stared down into Hamilton's red face. How easy it would be to kill him. Just a little more pressure…

"Would I lie to you now?" Hamilton gasped. "When my life is at stake? She left me. I swear, it's the truth."

"What about that list of undercover agents you say she stole? I suppose she just handed it over before she took off."

"Of course! She knew she had no choice, if she wanted me to hush things up."

Matthew's thumbs pressed deeper. Hamilton gurgled. This couldn't be the truth. Not about Mia…

And yet. And yet…

She'd left him without protest that night. Yes, she'd reversed the bit about the tattoos, but so what? It wasn't as if she'd gotten the theory of evolution wrong. Which tattoo he and his brothers had argued over wasn't exactly world-shaking.

"Matt?"

But that other thing she'd said. About the end justifying the means...

"Matt!"

He looked up. Alex and Cam were standing on either side of him.

"The Agency can get a lot out of him," Cam said softly. "Finish him off, what he knows about the cartel dies with him."

Training. Discipline. The code of honor Matthew lived by took over. He lifted his hands from Hamilton's throat and stepped back.

"I'm going to find her," he said, as much to his brothers as to their purple-faced prisoner.

"Fine. Just wait until the Agency cleanup crew arrives and we'll go with you."

Matthew shook his head. "I'm going alone."

"Matt. Wait for us. You don't even know where to start looking."

"I'm going alone," he said softly. "That's how it has to be."

The Knights waited for the cleanup crew.

They'd take care of everything, the way they always did.

An hour later, Matthew stood outside the colonel's house with his brothers. Cam rubbed his hands over his face and yawned. "What I need is a steak, a pot of coffee—and a plane home."

Alex nodded. "The same here."

They looked at Matthew.

"What I need," he said tonelessly, "are some answers."

"Matt," Cam said, "look, man, sometimes a thing just doesn't work out the way you hope, you know?"

"I have to know the truth."

"You mean—you mean, if she's—if she's dead…"

"She isn't." Matthew frowned, knowing how crazy he'd sound. "I'd know it, if she were."

"Yeah." Alex nodded. "Well, then, what Hamilton said. About her going with him willingly—"

"I know what he said."

"But you don't believe it."

Matthew hesitated. "I don't want to believe it."

Cam sighed. "Yeah. But that's not the same thing."

"No. It's not."

The brothers were silent. Then Alex spoke.

"Does she know your cell number? I mean, if she does and she hasn't contacted you…"

"She doesn't know the number." His jaw knotted. "But she knows my name. That I'm from Dallas."

The implications were clear. If Mia had wanted to reach him, she could have.

"In that case, man, come on home with us. Give this up. Write it off as—as just one of those things."

Matthew smiled at his brothers. "Is that what you'd do?" Their silence was all the answer he needed. "Come on," he said, wrapping his arms around their shoulders. "I'll buy you those steaks, put you on a plane—"

"Listen to him," Alex said. "Big talk, from a man who spent his last dollar buying toys from a thug named *amigo*."

"He's not a thug. And I've got a credit card."

"Yeah, yeah. Promises, promises…"

The brothers joked and laughed and spent the next

couple of hours together, carefully avoiding any discussion of Mia Palmieri until the last possible minute.

At the airport, their smiles faded.

"Be careful, okay?" Alex said.

Cam nodded in agreement. "Things get hairy, call us."

Matthew said he would. He smiled, gave them a thumbs-up, watched them board the Learjet for the flight home.

Then he got into his SUV and started driving the same route he'd taken in what felt like a different lifetime.

The route through the mountains, that would once again lead him to Mia.

He was sure of it.

If Hamilton had told him the truth, if Mia had gone, she'd want to go someplace safe. Someplace where she could plan her next steps without having to worry about the cartel or Hamilton or the authorities.

She'd be afraid to try to get back to the States. For all she knew, Hamilton or even the government would have her stopped.

There had to be a safe haven, a place Hamilton wouldn't think she'd go, a place the authorities didn't know existed.

Matthew could think of only one place like that.

I feel so safe here, Mia had said, of his house in the Cachalú.

And it would be safe. She was smart. She had to figure Hamilton would chalk it up as the last spot to look for her, assuming he was looking. Why would he expect her to return to the place where he'd found her the first time?

She had to figure, too, that Matthew had returned to the States. He'd done his job by finding her. Anyway, she could check easily enough. All it would take was a couple of phone calls. To the house, to his Dallas office.

He knew where she was. In the mountains. He could feel it in his bones. His Comanche bones, the ones that were still tied to the Old Ways.

Mia was in the Land of the Sky.

Soon, he would be there, too. He'd drive straight through. If his brothers were here, they'd say he was exhausted but hell, he was long past that.

Who needed sleep, when you were racing on adrenaline?

He'd find Mia. Ask questions. And if she didn't have the right answers...

If she didn't...

His hands tightened on the steering wheel.

He wasn't going to think about that now.

It was completely dark when he pulled off the main road and headed down the dirt track toward the house.

No lights shone in its windows.

The first bit of doubt crept into his mind. Maybe he was wrong. Maybe she wasn't here...

No. She was. She had to be. He knew it.

Matthew shut off his headlights. He drove a little farther, then pulled the SUV over and got out. He'd do the last half mile on foot. He was dressed for it, still wearing the black clothing he'd worn on the raid at Hamilton's place in Cartagena.

Something flew by his face; he felt the brush of its wings against his hair. Only the creatures of the night were out now; it was a time when hungry predators stalked unsuspecting prey.

His heart was beating fast. His breathing was shallow. This was how he'd always felt on night raids, excitement pumping through him, every sense alert.

He went up the steps quietly. Inserted his key in the front door. Slipped inside and quickly punched in the security code.

There was a flashlight in the desk in the library. He switched it on, kept the beam low, but there was no sign of her.

Wait. There was. Her scent was here. The aroma that always reminded him of a field of white flowers.

But she wasn't in the house. He checked all the rooms.

And then, he understood.

It wasn't the house where she'd felt safe. It was the forest clearing. The place where they'd made love so many times, where he'd realized he loved her…

Where he'd imagined he loved her.

A coldness crept into his bones. He turned off the flashlight, went out the sliding door to the deck and down the steps to the path that led through the trees.

Soon, he'd see Mia.

He'd ask her for the truth.

And then—God, and then, if he had to, he'd end this.

CHAPTER THIRTEEN

THE FOREST was dark.

The only sound was the roar of the waterfall.

The moon had risen, a fat, ivory globe that seemed suspended in the leafy branches of the trees. Its light illuminated the clearing and the jewel-like pool.

Illuminated Mia, standing naked under the frothy liquid veil of the waterfall.

He stood on the edge of the clearing, watching her and searching deep within himself for the discipline by which he'd lived his life, but that was the trouble.

He had no discipline when it came to her.

He'd searched for her, found her, then lost her.

Now, he had her trapped. She was his... Except, she wasn't. She'd made that clear. She had left him for another man. A man who wanted her back even though he said she had betrayed him.

Then, why would you want her? Matthew had asked, at the beginning.

It was an honest question. He'd understood that the woman would be beautiful—the man had shown him her photograph—but the world was filled with beautiful women. What made this one so special?

The man had looked embarrassed. He'd given a little laugh and said he wanted her back because she was more than beautiful.

She was, he'd said, everything a man could ever hope for.

Matthew felt his body quicken.

It wasn't true. She wasn't everything a man could hope for.

She was more.

He knew that now because, for a little while, she had belonged to him. She was Eve, she was Jezebel, she was Lilith reborn. She could be as wild as the summer lightning that streaked the hot sky or as sweetly gentle as spring rain.

Just looking at her was enough to stir a man's soul.

Her face was oval, her eyes wide-set and dark above an aristocratic nose and a mouth made for sin.

Her hair was long and dark as coffee. It tumbled down her back in a mass of curls that begged for his touch.

She was tall and slender, but her breasts were full and round. His breathing grew uneven at the thought of how they'd filled his hands.

And her legs…her legs were meant to clasp a man's waist. He could still remember the feel of them as he parted her thighs and sank deep, God, so deep into her heat.

Matthew shuddered.

God, was he losing his mind?

Who was Mia Palmieri? What was she? Was she his woman or Hamilton's? Had everything been a game?

All he knew right now was that she was a temptress.

But he was a warrior.

She swung toward him.

Matthew held his ground. She couldn't possibly see

him. He was still dressed in black, the kind of stuff he'd worn on night maneuvers in Special Forces and then in the Agency. He knew that he blended in against the tangle of night-shadowed forest behind him.

Did she somehow sense his presence?

Was that why she was tilting her head back, lifting her face to the curtain of water? Why she was raising her hands, cupping her breasts as if she were offering herself to the gods?

Offering herself to him?

He was hard as stone. So hard that it hurt.

Once, he had promised to return her to the man who'd sent him to find her.

Tonight, his only promise was to himself.

Slowly he stepped forward into the patch of moonlight that swathed the little clearing. He waited, muscles tensed, willing her to look toward him again. Why? Why not just call out and let her know he was here?

The answer was a cold whisper inside his head.

Because he wanted to see what she did when she saw him. Would she run to him? Throw herself into his arms? If she did—God, if she did…

But she didn't.

Her reaction was like a kick in the gut.

Her eyes widened. Her lips parted on a little exclamation of surprise. She flung one arm across her breasts, the other over her feminine delta in an age-old gesture of modesty.

He knew damned well it was reflex action and nothing more, knew he had all the answers he needed… the answers he hadn't wanted.

"No," she said.

He couldn't hear the word but he could see her mouth

form it. "No," she said again, and Matthew felt the swift rush of adrenaline as it coursed through his body.

His lips drew back in a predator's smile. He toed off his running shoes, pulled his shirt over his head, unzipped his trousers and stepped free of them.

Stood still, letting her see the full measure of his arousal.

Then he dove cleanly into the dark jungle pool and went for her.

Mia had come down the path to the pool with her senses on alert for the animals that hunted these woods at night.

But she was alone. Alone for the rest of her life, she'd thought...and then, suddenly, she'd felt a human presence.

Matthew, she'd thought, her heart soaring, even though she knew it was impossible.

Matthew was gone.

She'd come to his house because it was the only place she knew where she'd feel safe. Douglas would never think to look for her in the same place he'd already found her.

She'd prayed Matthew would still be here even though she knew better. Of course, he hadn't been. The house was empty. And yet, there were traces of him. A coffee cup, in the sink. His scent on the pillow in his bedroom.

She slept there, in his bed, holding the pillow in her arms.

A night passed. A day. And then, this evening, she'd felt—she'd felt something. A rift in time and space. Whatever it was, it had drawn her here, to the moonlit pool, the place where she and Matthew had made love.

Now, she sensed that she was being watched.

Had Douglas found her? Fear almost turned her legs to jelly…and then a figure materialized from the shadows.

Matthew.

Joy flooded her heart. He was here. The man she loved—but when she saw his face, so cold, so fierce, she knew that he still believed all Douglas's lies.

"No," she murmured.

He couldn't believe them. He had to give her the chance to explain.

"No," she said again, and as if he'd heard her, his lips turned up in a chilling smile.

It was a smile that suited what Douglas had told her about him, in excruciating detail.

"You lover is a killer," he'd whispered, holding her chin in his hand, angling her head up high enough to make breathing difficult. "He has blood on his hands."

He wasn't. Matthew wasn't a killer. He was gentle and loving and—

Oh God!

Transfixed, she watched as he stripped off his clothes. Stood straight and tall under her gaze. That chiseled face. The powerful body. The enormous, proud erection.

She began to tremble. There was nothing subtle in his message.

He wanted her to see him in all his primitive male savagery before he wreaked his vengeance on her.

Matthew dove into the pool.

Mia turned, scrambled up the water-slicked rocks, and began to run.

* * *

She was running. Running for her life.

Matthew stepped from the water. Good. He wanted her afraid. Terrified. Wanted her to know what it felt like to fear his retribution.

He waited until the trees swallowed her. He knew what lay ahead when the forest thickened. Brambles. A thicket of wild rose.

Nothing would slow him.

He'd been trained for running his quarry to ground.

Now he set off after her. He moved quickly, silently, avoiding the branches that reached out to snare him, dodging the brambles.

There. She was just ahead of him. He quickened his pace, closed the gap between them, caught her in his arms and spun her around. She was panting for breath; her hair was wild, and he told himself the swift surge of joy he felt was only what a hunter felt when he brought down his prey.

"Hello, Mia."

"Matthew." Her hands rose between them. She pushed at his shoulders. "Whatever you think—"

"Whatever I think, it's wrong. Is that what you were going to say?"

"Yes. Yes! I know how it seems. I know what Douglas said. But—"

"But he lied."

"Yes." She drew a sobbing breath. "He and I were never involved. How could I have slept with a man I despised, Matthew? How?"

"Maybe the same way you slept with me." His mouth twisted. "As if it were all part of a game you had to play and win."

"I *was* playing a game. With Douglas. Not with you. Never with—"

Matthew caught her hands and crushed them against his chest.

"Then, why didn't you tell me the truth? All you had to say was, 'Matthew, I'm on the run because I work for the Agency. I was sent to Cartagena to spy on Douglas Hamilton. That's why he wants me back. Because I'm a spy.'"

"How could I tell you that?" Her eyes met his. "I didn't know you. I didn't know anything about you, except that you were working for Douglas."

"I told you that I wasn't."

"But you were. He asked you to find me and take me back to him, and that's what you were doing. How could I trust you? How could I tell you the truth about me?"

It was a reasonable question but he wasn't in the mood for reason. It was hard enough holding Mia in his arms, feeling her naked body against his, inhaling her scent, without trying to deal in logic.

"I might buy that," he said roughly, "but then things changed between us." His mouth thinned. "A man expects a woman to be honest with him after he fu—"

Somehow, she wrenched her hand free. She hit him, her palm stinging his face.

"Don't you dare call it that," she said in a shaky whisper. "We made love. You know we did. It wasn't— it wasn't dirty or cheap or—"

Tears streamed down her cheeks. Let her cry, Matthew thought grimly. It wouldn't change a thing.

Except, it did.

Her sobs were wrenching. He'd seen women weep before, but never like this. If it was an act, his Mia deserved an Academy Award.

His Mia. His beautiful, courageous, incredible Mia.

"Don't cry," he said gruffly.

Mia shook her head. "I hate you," she said brokenly.

"Yeah. Just like you hate Hamilton."

Her head came up. The look she gave him, through tearstained lashes, was one he knew he'd never forget.

"Which do you want, Matthew, the truth—or the lies he told you?"

He didn't answer. Then he shrugged. "I'm listening," he said tonelessly.

"I was his secretary a few years ago, when he was stationed in Washington. The Agency figured he'd turned but they needed proof. Since I knew Douglas, they asked me to go to Colombia as his personal—"

"Assistant. I know all of that." Matthew's jaw tightened. "And then," he said softly, his eyes locked to hers, "you saw a way to make a killing. You could smuggle dope—"

"No!"

"And you could sell out the Agency and DEA people working undercover."

"No!" Mia pounded her fist against his chest. "Do you really think I could do that?"

Matthew looked into her eyes. Felt the warm softness of her in his arms. Something deep inside him seemed to crumble. It was, he thought with wonder, the wall he'd built around his heart.

"Do you?"

His arms tightened around her. "No," he whispered into her hair. "No, baby, I know you couldn't."

Mia caught her breath. "Matthew. Oh, Matthew…"

She lifted her face and he kissed her hungrily, tasting not just the sweetness of her mouth but the innate goodness of her soul.

"Tell me," he murmured. "Let it all out, sweetheart. I know what it's like to keep the ugliness inside."

She told him everything.

How Hamilton had stumbled across her leafing through his files. How he'd set her up so it looked as if she'd tried to smuggle cocaine.

"He held it over my head," she said, her voice shaking. "He said he'd have me locked away in a Colombian prison before I could even think about contacting anyone unless I reported back and told them they'd been wrong about him. He said—he said the only way I could guarantee I'd behave would be to sleep with him."

Matthew's vision reddened. *Hamilton,* he thought coldly, *Hamilton, you son of a bitch, I should have killed you.*

"I said I would, but I begged him to give me some time. The next morning, I broke into his computer, found a file that listed all his contacts in the cartel and at the embassy—"

"The embassy, too?"

She nodded. "That's why I didn't just send the list to Bogotá. I didn't know who I could trust. So I copied the list onto a miniature compact disk and took off."

"Just, took off. Without a destination in mind."

"All I knew was, I had to get away with that list." She gave a wobbly laugh. "I stashed the little CD in my compact."

God, she was wonderful! "That's brilliant."

"I just wonder what they're going to think at the Agency, when it arrives."

"You sent it to the Agency?"

Mia nodded. "Yesterday. Evalina came by. She

thought you were still here but... Well, I asked her if she knew where there was a Fed-Ex office."

Matthew shook his head in wonder. "And?"

"And she said there was one in the next town, that her husband drove by it every day on his way to work. So I put the compact into a padded envelope I found by going through your desk. I hope you don't mind."

"No," he said, trying not to smile, "I don't mind at all."

"Her husband dropped it off for me. Evalina brought me the receipt this morning."

Matthew gave her a long, deep kiss. "You're an amazing woman, Mia Palmieri." His arms tightened around her. "Let's go back to the house," he said softly. "I'll build a fire. You can tell me the rest after you're warm again."

"I'm fine," Mia protested, but he knew she wasn't. She was trembling; her skin was cool and damp. She was a heartbeat away from shock and he knew, without question, that if he lost this woman, his life would have no meaning.

He swept her into his arms, carried her through the moonlit night to the house. He wrapped her in a blanket, slipped on a pair of sweatpants and built a fire. Then he poured brandy for them both and drew her into his lap.

"I almost went crazy," he said gruffly, "when you let Hamilton take you away."

"I didn't have a choice."

"He threatened you, right?"

"Yes."

His voice hardened. "The bastard said he'd hurt you unless you went with him."

"No." She caught his hand in hers and pressed it to her heart. "He said he'd kill you," she whispered. "That he had other men, hidden in the dark, and they would—they would kill you if I didn't—if I didn't…"

Matthew cursed, drew her to him and kissed her again. His Mia was the most courageous woman he'd ever known. That she would have willingly sacrificed her freedom, her very life for him was a gift beyond any he could imagine.

"But I escaped."

"How?"

She giggled. It was such a nice, normal sound that Matthew grinned from ear to ear.

"Ah," he said. "You did something amazingly clever."

"Amazingly devious, you mean. We'd been driving for maybe half an hour. I was desperate." She leaned back in Matthew's arms. "See, there was this boy who lived next door, when I was maybe six or seven…"

"Don't tell me. He's my competition?"

Smiling, she looped her arms around his neck. "He was my very best friend. I wanted to do everything he did, so he taught me some stuff."

"What stuff?" Matthew felt his body starting to stir. His desire for Mia had been banked by the anguish of her story but now, with her safely in his arms, the hungry need he always had for her was coming back.

She knew it, too.

"Matthew," she said, shifting her weight in his lap. "Don't you want to hear how I got away?"

He gritted his teeth. "Yes. Yes, I do."

"Well, this boy next door…"

"Mia." Matthew swallowed hard. "Sit still."

"Why?" she said innocently. Then she laughed

softly and kissed him. "Okay. I'll be good. For a little while, anyway."

"What about this kid next door?" he said gruffly. "What'd he teach you?"

"Important things." She smiled. "How to catch fireflies. How to make water bombs."

Matthew chuckled. "A guy after my own heart."

"And he taught me how to burp."

"He what?"

"He taught me how to burp. You know, you swallow some air and then—"

"Yeah. I know." He kissed the tip of her nose. How had he ever gone through life without this woman beside him? "So, what's this have to do with getting away from Hamilton?"

"Well, we were riding in his car. In the back. And I was desperate. So I swallowed air. Lots of it. And then I let out this huge, disgusting burp and I made a gagging sound and I said, 'Ohmygod, Douglas, I have to throw up!'"

"You didn't," Matthew said, with unabashed delight.

Mia grinned. "He's very fastidious. He's a horrible, horrible man—but a fastidious one." She kissed Matthew's chin. "He told his driver to pull over. We were passing through one of those little towns the road runs through, you know?"

"And?"

"And, I got out of the car. I made some truly dreadful noises. Douglas backed away and I—I ran."

"Ran?" Matthew's smile faded. "Through the town? All through those back alleys in the dark?"

"I didn't have much choice," she said reasonably, and how could he argue when he knew she was right? "It took hours but I finally found my way back here."

Her voice trembled; the hint of laughter in her voice faded. "But you were gone. I kept praying you'd come back, but—"

Matthew silenced her with a kiss. "Mia," he said softly, framing her face with his hands, "do you remember the last night we were together? I told you I wanted to talk to you."

"And I said the same thing. I was going to tell you the truth. That I worked for the Agency. That I was spying on Douglas." She smiled into his eyes. "Because by then, I trusted you, Matthew. With my life." She paused. "With my heart."

"And I trust you with mine," he said softly. "It's what I wanted to tell you, that night." He took a deep breath. "I love you, Mia."

"Matthew." She kissed his mouth. "I love you, too."

"Will you marry me, Mia Palmieri?"

Her smile lit the room. "Yes. Oh, yes, my love, I will."

Their kiss was long and lingering. Mia shrugged and let the blanket fall from her shoulders.

God, Matthew thought, how exquisite she was.

He lifted her in his arms, carried her to the rug before the fireplace and lay down with her, watching the flames turn her hair to copper.

"You're beautiful," he said softly. "And brave. And mine, forever."

"Yours, forever," Mia sighed, and opened her heart, and her arms, to the man she adored.